SHRINK TO FIT

Dona Sarkar

SHRINK TO FIT

KIMANI
TRU
™

SHRINK TO FIT

ISBN-13: 978-0-373-83095-4
ISBN-10: 0-373-83095-5

www.KimaniTRU.com

Printed in U.S.A.

To my father, Shyamal, and to Manav, for never making me
feel as if I need to shrink (or anything else!) to fit.

Acknowledgments

Sha-Shana Crichton, this is our third year of working together and with each passing day, I am astounded at your incredible talent and effortless faith in me and my work. Thank you for everything.

Evette Porter, Linda Gill, Heather Foy and the rest of the Harlequin team, thank you for your continued support, dedication and freedom of creativity.

Fred Nava and Brendan Dohm, thanks for letting me make you evil! (And for always being there to listen to my rants, of course!)

My Microsoft friends and co-workers, I know you're not my target audience, but your enthusiasm for this endeavor of mine is worth more than a high school full of teenage girls! I don't have enough words to describe how honored I am to work with you every single day.

Tera Lynn Childs, Heather Davis, Simone Elkeles, Tina Ferraro, Marley Gibson, Stephanie Hale…the most talented group of YA writers I have ever met. It's been a tremendous year for all of us, and here's to many more years of Buzz Girl success!

Gordon Donnell, Pat Farrell, Erin Lotterl, Melanie Childers, thank you for your patience and critiques of this book.

My friends and family in Seattle, Detroit, India, California, England and around the world. Your strength and love keep me writing page after page.

Krish, Nabhan, Nabib, Joe and the Bay Area Crew, you guys are so amazing. Thanks for always keepin' it real.

Bonnie, Minal and Nisarga, if I had to create the ideal brothers and sisters, they wouldn't compare to you.

Mummy and Papa, for calling me your own from the very beginning.

My mom and dad, extraordinary people who keep believing long after I've given up. Thanks for never giving up.

And for the one who's there every single hour of every day, my husband Manav Mishra. To call what we share "love" is a discourtesy. You're my partner, my confidant, my best friend, my mentor…my everything.

one

Love and Basketball

Leah Mandeville poised her arms above her head, the ball weighing heavily in her sweaty palms. She glanced at the timer. Five seconds. The cheers of the girls' basketball fans, her teammates as still as action figures on the court, the cheerleaders suspended in a perfect pyramid—all waiting for her to make the perfect shot.

Leah lived for these moments. Nothing got her higher. Yeah, it was a cliché. Tall, big girl who was good at basketball. Every eye in the gym on her muscular body. Every breath held as they waited to see if Sonoma High School would finally be real contenders in girls' basketball that year.

Leah knew she could easily make this shot and get

it over with. But she loved the anticipation of the audience, the held breaths. She loved putting on this show. All eyes on her.

Gracefully, Leah arched the ball into the air, as dirty and orange as the trampled autumn leaves that had been tracked into the gym, toward the basket.

Fly.

Everything happened at once. The referee blew the whistle. The Sonoma fans stormed the court, and Leah, in the center of it all, was caught up in a mad group hug as Allison Taylor and Julia DeLouis swept her into the air.

Coach Jenna Richards was grinning ear-to-ear as she swung an arm around Leah's shoulders. "Nice one, Mandeville. Real nice."

"It's official, folks! Thanks to Leah Mandeville's tiebreaking three-point shot, Sonoma High School scores its first win of the season. Will Miss Mandeville be able to keep this up? Stay tuned...."

The words echoed in Leah's head as hot water pulsated through her shoulder-blade-length hair. She pumped a handful of the generic school shampoo (that smelled suspiciously like the generic hand soap all the sink dispensers were full of) out of the dispenser. Her mama had told her a thousand times to bring her own shampoo from home, "Indigo Bright, specially made for women of color." Apparently, anything less would cause Leah's coarse hair to gray early and fall out faster than the contestants on *American Idol*. Her mother, the almost-supermodel, had time to research these things. Leah did not. She scrubbed the generic stuff through her scalp and created a mound of frothy bubbles.

It had been a good game. Better than good. Incredible. The only thing that could have gone better would have been the second quarter. She'd missed an easy shot. If she'd scored that one, the game wouldn't have been so close. No one would be able to say she'd just gotten lucky at the end, as they surely would today.

Leah's self-criticism was interrupted by the rumble of her stomach. Perfect timing. The entire team was going to Slotki's for ice cream to celebrate the win. Leah was looking forward to her cake batter sundae with hot fudge. And whipped cream. And coconut sprinkles. What was life without coconut sprinkles? She watched the shampoo suds swirl, much like a mound of whipped cream, into the drain and wrapped a towel around her.

As Leah pulled a long-sleeved ringer tee over her head and tugged dark denim jeans over her hips, she frowned. Were her jeans feeling tighter? She sighed. Her mama would be on her butt if she went up any higher than a "respectable" size 8. Heaven forbid Leah cross into the double digits.

No matter. She wasn't your average teenage clothes-hanger-size girl, but her generous frame was all muscle. Well, most of it anyway. Plus, she highly doubted a normal high-school girl could pump out fifty push-ups and ten pull-ups in under three minutes.

"Honestly, darling, you are the last person who should be frowning like that," Allison Taylor drawled in her born-and-bred Bostonian accent as she finished blowing her hair straight. "Leah scores yet again. What complaints could you possibly have in life?"

"Thanks." Leah couldn't help but smile back. The blond senior could be an extra on *Veronica Mars* with her silky hair and whip-smart comebacks. As last year's star of the basketball team, she had given Leah a hard time about being a junior *and* the starting forward.

"I'm only saying it because you deserve it. This time anyway. Keep it up, huh?" Allison shot a sidelong glance at Leah. "Getting into the semifinals could really do wonders for the recruiting around here. Especially for juniors."

Meaning her.

"True that," Leah replied easily, not sure if she should take Allison's backhanded compliment as an insult or not. True, Leah wasn't your typical straight-A, valedictorian wannabe. But who needed that? Her goal was to play ball for UCLA in two years.

"Coming to Slotki's?" Allison wrapped the cord of her ionic jumbo-jet hair dryer and tossed it into her bag.

Leah glanced at her disheveled reflection. "I'll be out in three minutes."

And that's exactly, down to the second, how long it took Leah to get ready. She ran a brush through tangled, ebony hair, which would dry into a frizzy disaster if she left it alone. Not wanting to take that chance, she coiled it into her usual tight bun. A dab of tinted moisturizer to brighten up her ashy cocoa skin, and a slick of Smith's rosebud salve on her lips and lids, and Leah was ready to go.

Leah started tossing her lip gloss and hairbrush into her tote bag. That encounter with Allison had been almost…civil, compared to all their previous conversations. Funny, in eighth grade, she'd been friends with almost her entire class. Now, with so many cliques and interest groups forming the high-school food chain, she still didn't know where she fit in. Half her friends from middle school had become nerds and the other half had become cheerleaders. Neither hung out with the other. Or with her.

"Hey! Great game!" Shazan Ali tossed her perfectly highlighted chocolate and caramel hair behind her shoulders and made pouty fish lips into the mirror as she plunked her makeup bag down next to Leah.

She'd changed out of her cheerleading outfit into a long-sleeved minidress.

"What the hell did you do to your hair? Did your mom see this yet?"

"Please." Shazan rolled her eyes. "If she had it her way, I would be wearing a friggin' burka to school every day. With this cute Forever 21 stuff underneath!"

Shazan had once told Leah that Muslim women who wore burkas, the full-black head-to-toe graduation gown-type thing, also wore totally slutty clothes underneath. Microminis and belly-baring tank tops. Stuff Shazan strutted around in on a daily basis, much to the chagrin of her family.

"C'mon, Shazzam." Leah referred to her friend by her grade-school nickname. "A burka? Maybe a hijab, but not the full-on storm-trooper outfit."

"Shut up." According to Shazan, covering up two-hundred-dollar highlights with hijabs, the pretty, colorful head scarves her mother wore, was a crime of fashion (not to mention sanity).

"Was Queen Allison actually talking to you?"

"Yeah. Weird, right? She came over to tell me I did good today. I think so anyway."

Shazan raised a perfectly threaded eyebrow. *As if,* her look seemed to say.

Julia DeLouis, Allison's best friend, was still curling

her hair, not even five feet away. Leah lowered her voice a notch. "Maybe she's okay."

Shazan didn't bother. "Don't listen to anything that bitch says. Everything has two meanings. At least."

"I'll wait and see."

Shazan rolled her eyes. "I warned you. You're so gullible sometimes, Leah."

Ah, the not-so-secret rivalry between the jocks and the cheerleaders. Leah and Shazan had been friends since second grade. Two peas in a pod. Until high school, that was. Shazan had suddenly discovered the fizzy world of cheerleaders and the cute footballer boys they usually dated. Leah was suddenly all alone and had turned to basketball and discovered she was actually pretty good at it. She and her former best friend often found themselves at opposite ends of the clique divide.

Shazan deftly applied green eye shadow to her wide-set brown eyes and brushed bronzer on her already tanned cheeks. "Remind me to wash this stuff off before I go home. *Amma* flipped last week when she found my stash of MAC lip glosses. I said they were yours."

"Great." Leah grabbed one of *her* so-called MAC lip glosses and squeezed a drop onto her fingertips. Sparkly lavender. It would look so stupid on her while transforming her friend into Abercrombie model material.

It amazed her sometimes that people used to mistake her and Shazan for sisters when they had been younger. Since then Leah had shot up over a foot and was still growing into her arms and legs while Shazan had shrunken into the required size 2 for the "popular" girls.

Somehow, they'd remained friends. Whether it was because Shazan still liked hanging out with her, or needed her vote to become Snow Ball Princess, was beyond Leah, but she liked to believe the former.

"So, what are you doing this weekend?" Shazan continued to hunt around in her Clinique makeup bag. She came up with a scary metal-looking contraption that she used to pinch her eyelashes.

"Um, not much. Hanging with Jay, I guess. Hoops. I might let him win for once," Leah said, wincing as Shazan lined the inside of her lower eyelid with eyeliner. Ouch.

"Ohhh…" Shazan caught Leah's eye in the mirror. "Jay, huh? Still?"

Now it was Leah's turn. "Shut up."

"Are you ever going to tell him?"

"Tell him what? We're friends. That's it."

"Whatever."

Leah's cheeks warmed. She was lousy with secrets. That was why it was extra important Jay never even got a hint.

"God, you have *such* good skin," Shazan commented, losing interest in Leah's love life and moving on to examining a nonexistent spot on her perfectly smooth cheek. "Mine is, like, freaking Crater Lake."

"A gift from my mama," Leah said, hiding a smile. The more beautiful Shazan became, the more issues she found to complain about. Last week, she had claimed she was fat and needed to be a size 0 by month's end to fit into some "totally perfectous" gown for the Snow Ball that December.

Shazan tossed her makeup into her bag and grabbed a pillbox. "You're so lucky she's a model. She meets the most amazing people. Didn't she get her *Vogue* cover done by Annie Leibovitz?"

The overhead fluorescent light bounced off the highlighter on Shazan's sharp cheekbones, which seemed to be more defined than usual.

"I don't even know who the hell that is." Leah eyed Shazan's pillbox. This was new. Her friend had never been sick a day in her life. Vitamins, maybe.

"Leah. God." Shazan shook out a pill. "You know you could totally be a model, too. Your mom would be your in. I'm dying to have a portfolio made, but my parents would kill me. Or ship me back to Pakistan. I'm not even kidding."

Well, that would officially be the first time anyone had ever been jealous of her. Especially Miss Popularity herself. Shazan was the shoo-in for Snow Ball Princess that year, the title given to the most beautiful junior-class girl.

Leah decided to forgo mentioning that she, herself, had no interest in posing for a camera, wearing next to nothing. Instead, her dreams involved becoming the most talented Bruin in UCLA women's basketball history. Still, it felt nice to be envied for once.

"You want one?" Shazan downed her pill without water and held up the box to Leah.

Leah raised an eyebrow as she took one. "Don't tell me this is birth control. I got no need for it. Yet."

A few of the other girls turned their heads as Shazan's wind-chime laughter rang out. "Me and Bill aren't *that* serious yet! They're diet pills. I need to lose those ten pounds. There is, like, no way in hell I can be Snow Ball Princess being the size of a horse like I am." She patted her flat stomach. "Plus, they give you an amazing caffeine boost. I take, like, three a day."

Diet pills? Leah had always thought they were dangerous. And addictive. But then, what did she know? Shazan seemed to be in excellent health. And thin as a stick at that.

"We better get going." Leah stuck the tiny pill into the back pocket of her jeans. Was Shazan implying that *she* was the "size of a horse" as well? She took one last look at herself in the mirror. Maybe she could afford to lose a few pounds. After all, "fitting the mold" had gotten Shazan in with the cool crowd and a really hot boyfriend.

As Leah followed Shazan out of the girls' locker room, her stomach growled again. Diet, schmiet. That could wait till tomorrow. She would get extra hot fudge on her sundae today.

"God, how do you eat like that!" Shazan pushed the dish of fat-free frozen yogurt toward Jennifer Chan after having taken exactly three tiny nibbles. "I'm totally done."

Leah dipped her spoon into her now-empty sundae dish and scraped the edges for remnant hot fudge slicks. She shrugged, feeling slightly proud. This reminded her of when she and her favorite cousin, Matt, used to have eating contests when they were kids. She would whup the pants off him every time. Hot dogs, ice-cream sandwiches, coconut cream pies…Matt named it, Leah ate it.

"She's totally something else, right?" Jennifer dipped her spoon into the austere vanilla frozen yogurt she was sharing with Shazan. "Must be where she gets the strength to make those kick-ass jump shots, right, girls?"

Mansa and Shobna, two other members of the cheerleading squad that sometimes hung out with them, had forgone ice cream altogether and were sipping diet sodas through straws. Leah frowned. What the heck was the point of an "ice-cream social" if she was the only one eating ice cream?

She glanced at where the basketball players were sitting. All of them were wolfing down strawberry sundaes and Jamocha shakes. Maybe she belonged with them. If only they had invited her to sit with them, that was.

Leah swore the only reason she actually had some semblance of a social life was Shazan. The remnants of their old friendship seemed to be getting her through high school.

"I was just a little hungry," she said.

"You should be. Your game was really on today." Jennifer fluffed her baby-doll bangs with her fingers and turned to stare at Leah's empty dish. "It's really cool that you don't obsess about all that sugar and fat going directly to your thighs."

Ouch. Leah stopped scraping at her dish. Was that supposed to be an insult? She glanced down at her thighs. They looked okay. But then again, Jennifer's thighs were about as tiny as Leah's wrists.

"Oh my God! Jenn, shut up!" Mansa squealed.

Leah breathed in relief. Finally, someone normal.

"I would trade your thighs for my arms any day!" Mansa continued as she gestured toward the underside of her arm. "See that jiggle? I feel like my grand-mother. And my butt? Could it *get* any bigger?"

Leah looked closely at Mansa's offensive arm, but she saw nothing except taut caramel-colored skin and a tiny freckle.

"Have you guys tried that new cellulite cream by L'Oréal? It's totally supposed to get rid of that nasty stuff on your thighs in like six weeks!" Shazan forgot all about her frozen yogurt and started rummaging in her bag. "I thought I had it somewhere…"

Leah set her spoon down immediately. Cellulite? What the heck was cellulite? It sounded contagious. She certainly didn't want to catch it.

She was suddenly knocked out of her chair with a sharp jab in between her shoulder blades. "I see you're drinking one percent. Is that 'cause you think you're fat? 'Cause you're not. You could be drinking whole milk if you wanted to."

Leah had never been so grateful for a shoulder-blade bruise.

She spun around to face a pair of impish black eyes and answered reflexively. "*Napoleon Dynamite*."

"Said by?"

"Napoleon!"

"Score." Jay Dalal grinned. Leah's best friend and verbal sparring partner. They shared a love of basket-ball, cooking pasta and movie quotes, always trying to one-up each other in all three categories. She was surprised he was talking to her in front of the cheerleaders. He couldn't stand any of them, especially Shazan. He was convinced the squad had the combined IQ of bread.

"Hey." Jay nodded in Jennifer Chan's direction casually. Except for one.

Jennifer gave him a flirtatious smile. "Haven't seen you in a while."

"Call you tonight," Jay murmured, barely audible to anyone else.

Jennifer raised an eyebrow and giggled. Leah froze. Was this actually getting serious?

She caught Shazan's eye from across the table. Her friend smiled sympathetically and shrugged.

It'll never last, her mischievous eyes seemed to say. Better not.

"Leah, you need a ride home or what?"

Leah's stomach burned and suddenly she felt the overwhelming desire to chuck Shazan's now-melted frozen yogurt at the back of Jay's head. He was such a hypocrite. First he complained that all of Leah's new friends were ditzes and bimbos. Then he went and fell for one of them, shoving Leah to the wayside.

"I'll see you guys tomorrow," she called to the girls as she followed Jay out to the car.

"Jackass," she mumbled under her breath, not knowing if she was talking to Jay or herself.

"What'd you say?" Jay pushed his sunglasses over his eyes and beeped to find his car in the lot, his worn-out flip-flops swishing on the hot sidewalk.

"Nothing," Leah muttered.

"Come over for dinner tonight. Ma's making tikkas. The lamb ones you like." Jay opened the car door for her. Ever the gentleman.

She hated him sometimes. The way he made unruly black hair, an American Eagle T-shirt and a pair of cargo shorts look cool instead of sloppy. The way he looked at her with one eye half narrowed as if he was trying to read her mind. The way he never looked at her quite the way she looked at him.

Jay had moved to Sonoma the first year of high school. He was sprawled casually on the bleachers in gym class the first day of school their freshman year and had made a sideways comment that girls couldn't throw. Leah had instantly challenged him to a game of one-on-one, managed to kick his ass without trying and after discovering they lived across the street from each other, had been friends ever since.

And then just to ruin everything, sometime in between the Homecoming Dance where they'd gone together as friends, and Jay's first date with Jennifer, Leah had suddenly and painfully fallen in love with him. Now she couldn't look at Jay without imagining how his well-defined lower lip would feel pressed against hers. Or his hands on her—

She blushed again and forced her attention to what Jay was saying as he started the car. Jay had gone out with Jennifer twice already and, from the looks of today, would be seeing her again that weekend. She had to forget about it. Their friendship wasn't worth ruining over some stupid crush.

"You coming to dinner or what?"

"Of course I am. Tell your mom she'll get someone who really appreciates her food tonight."

Jay flicked her cheek. "Jackass."

One day he would realize they were meant to be together. It was like that song, "Save the Best for Last." Eventually he would realize that he always came to her with his girl troubles and what he was looking for was right in front of him.

Someday anyway.

But for today, Jay Dalal was nothing more than her next-door neighbor and best friend and she would have to deal with that.

two

"Lynnette, you better be home!" Leah heard her mother's voice brimming with excitement as the front door slammed.

Lynnette. Leah hated being called her full name. It wasn't her. Never had been. Probably never would be. "Lynnettes" were always petite blond valedictorians who did volunteer work on weekends at the Humane Society and watched their carbs at mealtime. Like the Lynnette on *Desperate Housewives* with the kids and the job and the husband and the friends. Puke. Certainly not female basketball players who spent the evening munching on Choco Pies out of the box with her cat Espresso Bean and watching reruns of *Alias* instead of doing biology homework.

Leah hit the Pause button on the DVD player. Sydney Bristow had just been about to diffuse a bomb and save SD-6 from Quentin Tarantino. She would have to pause Sydney and superhottie Vaughn in the midst of their sizzling chemistry to see what her mother was giddy about.

"Living room, Mama." Leah shooed Espresso Bean off the couch. Her mama hated cat hairs on the furniture and had threatened to send Beanie to the pound more than once. But Leah had rescued the ratty old brown cat from a Dumpster last year and had fallen in love with her instantly.

Victoria Mandeville swept into the room and deposited a large sea-foam-colored shopping bag onto the leather couch.

"I have news." Her mother's eyes gleamed even brighter than their usual amber-gold as she kissed Leah on both cheeks. "You'll never guess what."

"You met Snoop Dogg." Leah reached for the bag. What had her mother brought her this time? "Oh, Mama. No!"

Leah held up a cobalt-blue dress with a fluttery bias-cut skirt. She would be a whale in this dress. An ashy whale at that. The dress was something her forty-five-year-old, Tyra Banks–look-alike mother would look stunning in, but not Leah. Never Leah. Bright colors completely washed out Leah's complexion, but made her mother glow—like every other color.

"Much better than Snoop Dogg, right?" Victoria grabbed the dress and flicked it in the air in front of Leah, like a bullfighter. "Listen, *Jade* magazine has a benefit in a few months for ozone-layer protection at the NELL. The agency would like to send me, of course, but they also asked for you. This is the dress you'll wear."

NELL? Natural Environmental Something Library? Her mother's modeling agency, Artisan Faces, was really trying to go the California one-with-the-earth route, sending their top models to these things. The agency was run by the extremely fashionable and social-savvy Alfreddo Riviera, who had glared at Leah disdainfully at the last benefit when during dinner she'd dared to actually finish her steak. Why on earth would he request Leah's presence again?

"Uh, is this another tree-hugging protest thing where there'll be no tree hugging *or* protesting?" Leah reached for the remote control again. The last good-for-the-earth benefit she'd attended with her mother had had nothing to do with saving dolphins or trees. Instead, skinny women had stood around in clusters discussing shoes and rich husbands, not to mention gossiping about who looked pregnant and who obviously had had a little "something something done."

Leah had spent the evening next to the buffet table sneaking cookies and trying every single kind of dessert, much to her mother's chagrin.

"We are absolutely going to go to this one." Victoria slapped the remote out of Leah's hand. "In January's issue of *Jade*, there's a special on mothers and daughters. You and I are going in be in that issue. It's your 'in' into the modeling world, I'll make sure of that."

Leah raised an eyebrow. Was her mother planning to birth and raise another daughter to adulthood in the next few months? Because that was the only way Victoria had any chance of being in the shoot.

"You won't believe some of the famous mother-daughter combos that *Jade* will be photographing. I'm talking Goldie and Kate, Kathy and Paris, Demi and Tallulah…"

Tallulah? Who named their kid Tallulah?

"Mama, please." Leah rolled her eyes and stood up. She knew her mother had dreams of having a daughter who was poised, beautiful and, above all, thin to follow in her graceful footsteps. But Victoria had to realize by now that Leah was not that person.

"Plus, they're going to take *one* nonfamous duo." Victoria ignored her and continued gushing, the platinum bracelets on her wrists jangling as she tugged at her perfectly pressed hair. "All the mothers in the agencies around L.A. are dragging their daughters to the gala to make a good impression on the *Jade* people. This is our big break! Can you imagine what it will do to my career if we're on the same page as Kate and Goldie? Not to mention yours! You and I, mother-daughter modeling combo who look like sisters. It'll be awesome!"

Leah wrinkled her nose. *Awesome?*

"You mean badass. Awesome is, like, 1997 or something."

"Fine, it'll be badass. We need to do something about your hair. I'm sure Ramon can—"

"I got bio to do. Why don't you go adopt someone? Get Shazan. She'd love to do it." Leah patted her mother's shoulder. "Nice try, but I'm too big. And not interested."

Victoria rested a hand on her hip. "This is *your* big break, little girl. We need to start thinking about your future. You and I have a chance to work with the best and we are going to take it. Now, I'm pulling the mom card. You're going and you're going to like it!"

"I'm going to be a basketball player. For UCLA. Isn't that right, Beanie? A basketball player!" Leah scooped Beanie into her arms. The cat rolled into a ball and started to purr. "That's right. Your mama is going to kick ass on the courts. Yes, she is."

"You're too beautiful to not be a model, okay? It's in your genes." Victoria wrinkled her nose at the cat, who glared in her direction.

"You're obviously nuts," Leah grumbled as the phone rang, interrupting the tirade she had been about to unleash.

"Watch your mouth, young lady. Do not make me wash your mouth out with soap."

"No one says that anymore either. How are you ever going to be cool without learning what's up?" Leah reached across the kitchen counter and grabbed her cell phone before Victoria could retort.

Jay's name showed on the caller ID. Her hero.

"Leah?"

"No, your mama." She did another eye roll. Was stupidity contagious today?

"Ha, ha. Gotta minute?"

Leah turned her back to her mother. His tone was serious. "Yeah, uh, it's fine. What up?"

"Just talked to Jenn."

"Who?"

"Jennifer. Jennifer Chan. Cheerleader. Valedictorian. Asian. Pretty—"

"Yeah, yeah, I get it. What about her?" Leah's smile disappeared. Of course. She was the sounding board for all of Jay's girl woes. Whenever he was serious, there had to be a girl involved.

"I want to ask her to the Snow Ball."

Leah's breath caught and the first word that flew out of her mouth was "Why?"

Jay was silent.

"Uh, I mean, why now? It's, like, thr-three months away," Leah stuttered, mentally slapping herself. If she kept this up, there was no way she could keep her feelings a secret. And if any of the cheerleaders were to find out or the basketball players, she would have to change schools to get away from the laughter.

"I know, I know. It's months away. But you know. I don't want her to go with someone else. Can you do me a favor?"

Leah grabbed Beanie before the cat had a chance to jump up on the kitchen counter where a carton of ice cream was melting. *Say no. Say no. Say no.* "Sure, what?"

God, she was a wuss. One of these days she was going to get up enough of a spine to say a firm "no!" to her mother and "I love you and always will" to Jay. That day was obviously not today.

"Can you find out if Jenn's going with someone already?"

"Jay, it's October. I doubt someone has reserved her already."

"Still, could you?"

"Fine," Leah muttered, chomping on her fingernails to keep the sarcasm out of her voice. "But if she thinks I'm asking her out, I'm gonna kick your ass."

"Thanks, babe."

Babe. The tone he said the flirtatious word with was anything but flirtatious.

"Pick you up in the morning?"

"Sure. Whatever." Leah hung up and studied her broken and bleeding nail, surprised by her anger at him. They'd been friends for three years. How was he supposed to know she wanted a change of status quo? It wasn't as if she had told Jay her feelings. Or even hinted at them. If she was thin and beautiful and smart…yeah, she would have told him by now. She stared down at her bloated stomach. But not like this.

Leah set her cell phone back into the charger.

"Lynnette."

"Mama, I'm really not in the mood." Leah set Beanie back on the floor and dropped down beside her. She rubbed the cat's belly. At least this little creature loved her just the way she was.

"Why don't you tell him how you feel, huh? He's always up in here. He's got something for you. It's obvious."

Leah's cheeks burned as she stood up. There went the theory that she'd been discreet. Shazan knew. Her mom knew. It was only a matter of time before Jay found out, too.

"You won't understand, Mama. He likes those thin little cheerleader girls. Like Jennifer." Leah flopped down on the couch again.

"She pretty?" Victoria folded the blue dress and set it inside the bag.

"Yeah."

"Pretty as you?" Her mother leaned her elbows on the headrest of the couch and stared at Leah.

"Much more so."

"That's just not possible. Look at you! Those eyes, this hair…and, God, girl, your height!" Victoria carefully undid Leah's hair out of its usual bun. "You're made for modeling."

"Being tall doesn't make a girl a model," Leah muttered, sinking back into the couch.

"And why not? Alfreddo saw you at the Glamouratti Gala last month and asked if you were a model! He was all kinds of convinced."

Leah raised her eyebrow. She seriously doubted her mother's boss, the man who had discovered models that regularly walked the runways in Milan, girls with names like Lissandra and Kennedy, found her beautiful.

Leah gave her mother a look. "His exact words please?"

Victoria's voice was barely audible. "…size modeling or something like that."

Leah's face stung. Plus-size modeling? Modeling for fat girls?

Suddenly, she felt nauseated. Maybe the Choco Pies hadn't been the best idea.

"It was that dress. I told you empire waist didn't suit you. Did you listen to me, little girl? No, you didn't."

"Yeah, it must've been the dress. Couldn't have been my fat ass." Funny, she'd never thought of herself as fat. Just big-boned. Maybe she'd been in denial all these years.

She was good at sports, funny, decently smart. Yet she didn't have a boyfriend or a posse of friends as Shazan did. The day Shazan became tiny, her life changed. Maybe the same thing could happen for Leah.

"Come on, baby. If you lost, like, ten pounds, you could easily wear anything you wanted." Victoria seemed to be reading Leah's mind, while stroking her scalp. "You just need that extra confidence. I bet that boy would notice you in no time if you were on the cover of *Jade* magazine."

Victoria was manipulating her. That was obvious. But she seemed to have a point.

Leah's eyes fell on the various pictures around their house. Her beautiful mother…and her. Dumpy, fading-into-the-background her. Not being "pretty" had never bothered her before. But why shouldn't she have everything the other girls had?

If it was just ten pounds keeping her from having it all, why not go for it?

"I'll think about it. I gotta do homework." Leah scooped Espresso Bean over her shoulder and started to head to her room. "But don't count on me. Find another daughter. A thin one."

"Tried and failed. Back to you, little girl," Victoria called up the stairs.

Leah wasn't sure if she was kidding or not.

That night, Leah couldn't concentrate on algebra. Her mother's, Shazan's and Jay's words all swirled around in her brain. Snow Ball. Ten pounds. Diet pills. Size of a horse.

That's it.

Leah held her breath as she stepped on her mother's scale.

Two hundred pounds.

Yeah, that *was* heavy. That was heavier than most of the guys she knew. It probably wasn't even healthy.

From tomorrow on, no more junk food, no more sitting around after school. Hell, maybe she would go to the gala. If she could manage to not look like the Marshmallow Man in the skinny blue dress, that was. She had two weeks. Who knew? With enough hard work, maybe she would get up enough nerve to ask Jay to the Snow Ball.

She would diet like the other girls and maybe soon

she would actually look like them. Leah reached into her pocket and pulled out the shiny pink pill Shazan had given her. She set the pill on the edge of her tongue and swallowed without even a glass of water.

Everything would be different soon. She would show everyone.

three

Misery
198 lbs

"HEY! You look different. That shirt doesn't make you look as pretty as usual." Leah grinned as she slid into the passenger seat of Jay's silver Mustang. "Ah, never mind. It was just the light. You're still freaking metro."

"'I have to warn you, young lady, I am susceptible to flattery.'" Jay raised an eyebrow, his question obvious.

"*Kill Bill*," Leah answered automatically.

"Volume?"

"Two."

"Said by?"

"Esteban…Vihaio?"

"Very good." Jay tugged at Leah's long braid. "Glad to see you still have half a brain after being around the ditz squad."

"Wow, Jay. Original," Leah snarked back. "Ditz squad?"

He was planning on asking the queen of the ditz squad out. Men were ridiculous.

Jay glanced over at her. "Are you wearing a dress? What, you have a date with that tutor nerd or something?"

Leah punched him in the shoulder, her heart thudding. No, not for Alan Li. The freshman genius kid who tutored her in math had a very obvious fascination with her, but she didn't think of him that way. She was a foot taller than he and weighed three times as much. Besides, she only had eyes for one person.

Jay glanced at her, curiosity obvious on this face. "No, really. What's going on?"

She sighed, not wanting to admit the truth. The sleeveless black Victoria's Secret sheath had secret panels that held "everything in" according to her mother. Leah had stood in front of the mirror and scrutinized her stomach and butt from all angles and after about ten minutes, was convinced the dress did seem to smooth out bulges. But then, she didn't know if the flatter stomach was due to the smoothing panels or from skipping dinner the previous night after her newfound resolution.

"Laundry day. It was just sitting there in my closet," Leah muttered. She was a terrible liar. And she usually shared everything with Jay. Almost everything anyway.

Jay turned off her street and onto Peachtree Avenue. Everyone outside California considered Los Angeles to be glamorous and exciting. Actually, the city was plagued by poverty and corruption. An even split between people in the entertainment industry and the working class, the latter getting the shaft in the deal.

As they stopped at a light, Leah watched a homeless man hold out his hand to a bleached-blond waitress as she exited a diner, looking exhausted. She reached into her ragged denim bag and pulled out a few bills, no doubt her tips from the night before. Leah swallowed as she watched the waitress drop the money into the man's hands and his gap-toothed smile in return for her generosity.

Just one mile from her Hollywood Hills home, Leah mused, there were so many people who had problems much worse than not fitting into a four-hundred-dollar dress. She was being ridiculous. Twenty-four hours ago she hadn't given a damn what anyone thought of her. Now she was starving herself for some stupid gala she didn't care about.

But also for the dance. The Snow Ball. She remembered Victoria's words. *If you lost, like, ten pounds, you could easily wear anything you wanted... I bet that boy would notice you in no time if you were on the cover of* Jade *magazine.*

Leah glanced at the diner's window. Sausage, Eggs and Toast: $3.99. Her stomach growled. Breakfast had been a protein shake (Victoria's low-carb, low-fat protein powder) with skim milk and one strawberry. Lunch was going to have to be a salad. A big salad.

"Hey, you want to get out of here at lunch and go to In-N-Out?" Jay asked as Sonoma High School appeared at the end of Peachtree Avenue. "I'll buy you a shake."

"I can't eat that stuff!" As soon as Leah heard the words come out of her mouth, she regretted them. He was going to freak.

Jay hated when girls talked about how fat they were and were diet-obsessed. He made fun of the "Weight Equal to IQ" crowd and always told Leah she should never become like one of them.

"Excuse me?" As predicted, Jay's eyebrows shot up.

Leah avoided his eyes. "I, uh, my mom wants me to do some modeling shoot thing with her. I need to lose some weight first, though. Whatever."

Jay pulled the sleek car into a compact parking

spot. "She always wants you to do stuff like that. When are you going to tell her it's not your thing?"

Leah bit her lip. "Well, this one sounds pretty cool. I mean, there's Kate and Demi and—"

Even as Leah said the words, she realized how lame they sounded coming from her. "It'll be cool. I've never done anything like it before. First time for everything and all. But I really need to get my ass in gear and shed ten pounds."

Jay slowly pulled the keys out of the ignition. "Well, I guess you could lose a few."

Leah felt as though he'd slugged her. *She could lose a few?* He, too, felt she was fat? She'd expected him to tell her to shut up and that she was perfect the way she was. Obviously not.

"I mean, I'll help you work out and stuff if you want. I mean, the guys on the team—"

Leah felt her face start to flush red and didn't hear the rest of what he was saying. Jay, her best friend, the one guy whose opinion she valued was even ready to help her lose weight. She flashed back to Jay's last girlfriend. The tiny, ninety-five-pound Kanishtha. That was what he liked. Girls he could wrap his arms around. No matter how much fun he made of those girls, that was what he liked. That was what the whole world liked.

Her weight was obviously the reason they weren't

together. If she was thin, she would have him. She would be everything Shazan was.

Leah scowled as she opened the door to the passenger side. "I gotta go." Her voice, thankfully, was clear. She was doing the right thing. The food thing was going to be a pain, but she would get used to it. The payoff was too good to pass up.

"Hey, Leah!"

"Hmm?" She tried her best to keep her voice from breaking. "Yeah?"

"Meet me in the weight room before practice, huh? I need a spotter. And so do you. And lay off those sundaes. You'll lose what you need to in no time!"

"Mmm." Leah cursed under her breath. Forget sundaes. She would lay off *all* food for a while. And in two weeks when she unveiled her new body, everyone would be shocked—her mother, the cheerleaders, that lousy Alfreddo guy. And especially Jay.

Leah's heart pounded in time to her footsteps. *Rat-rat-rat.* Like the grillers at Mongolian BBQ pounding meat and vegetables into a scrumptious dish. Her stomach growled. Food—what she wouldn't give for a hot, spicy meal right about now. Barbecued beef with sesame oil, garlic, ginger and that killer hot sauce they used. Leah shoved the thought out of her head. Hot, spicy, scrumptious meals were what had gotten her where she was at that moment.

Damn. She had to stop thinking about food.

Her stomach growled again. A salad and the protein shake. That was all that was keeping her going. She couldn't believe she'd skipped her last class of the day for this. For this torture. She'd been sitting in geometry and all she could focus on was the roll of fat around her waist and her rumbling stomach. Unable to get the vision of herself as a laughingstock at the modeling gala out of her head, she faked a headache and asked to go to the office to lie down. Instead, she snuck down to the weight room.

She wasn't that great of a student, and she'd skipped class plenty of times. Usually it was to go to the beach or shoot hoops. Never to run on a treadmill like an obsessive cheerleader.

She pried her eyes off the distance counter on the treadmill: 2.70 miles. Felt as though she'd been trying to cross the three-mile mark for hours. "A watched treadmill timer never climbs," she chanted as she watched the clock on the wall, the random episode of *Oprah* on the wall-mounted television. Anywhere but at the distance counter.

Now 2.75 miles.

She snapped her eyes off the counter. Maybe it was broken. There was no way she'd only run .05 miles in the past forever. Maybe she should stop. Jay would be down here any minute. And she still had basketball practice after that. She started to reach for the emergency stop button. No need to have a heart attack on the first day of the Plan.

"'Tomorrow will be the most beautiful day of Raymond K. Hessle's life. His breakfast will taste better than any meal you and I have ever had.'"

Leah's heard swiveled when she heard a familiar voice quote the familiar line. *"Fight Club,"* she gasped.

"Said by?" Jay asked, circling around the line of treadmills to lean on the arm of Leah's. "Think fast."

"Agh. Um…"

"Five. Four. Three. Two…"

"Brad Pitt!" Leah burst out with her last breath.

"Good job. Hey, whoa. You did three miles already? How long have you been here?"

Leah hit the emergency stop button as she felt her knees giving out. Three miles. Finally. Three miles in thirty minutes. A personal best. Distraction. All she had needed was a good distraction. Maybe she should have Jay quiz her on movie quotes during *all* her workouts. That seemed to work. She'd barely felt the last three minutes.

Yeah, right.

As if Jay had nothing else to do but watch a chubster try to lose weight. She spurted a shot of water from her bottle onto her face to keep from staring at him. He looked too good. He always did these days.

Perfectly toned and tan in an oversize basketball jersey and navy shorts. Every day she wondered what had taken her so long to notice him. If she hadn't waited for so long, maybe, just maybe, she would have had a chance before.

"Three miles. Big deal," Leah panted as she grabbed the towel off the arm of the treadmill and swiped her face.

"Yeah, right. Look at you, Marion Jones." Jay laughed. "Come on. You need more water before we lift."

Leah shook her head. "I'm not as much of a wuss as you, Little Miss Sunshine."

"'Pfft! What's the matter, smart-ass, you don't know any fuckin' Shakespeare?'"

"The Departed." Leah recognized the line immediately. Jay had forced Leah to watch that movie three times on opening weekend. Not that she'd minded. During the especially bloody scenes, she'd buried her face in Jay's shoulder, pretending to be grossed out. It was a typical girl move, but, hey, she wanted to be a typical girl.

They'd gone into the theater as friends and when they came out, Leah couldn't stop thinking about Jay's comforting hand on her knee.

"You're good. You might even be better than me." Jay smirked. "Either you have a great memory, or a hell of a lot of free time."

"Both." Leah grinned.

"Shows."

"Smart-ass."

What Leah loved most about Jay was he seemed to be the only person who really "got" her. He got her humor and her moods. He also got the fact that she didn't act different around guys and girls. She was only comfortable with people when she was ribbing them, or being ribbed back.

"Think you can keep up with me, princess?" Leah teased as she tucked her towel into the back of her shorts and stretched out her arms. "Don't want you to break any nails."

Jay smirked as he led her to the weight corner. "Catch." He tossed her a thirty-pound bar, which she caught easily. "Not bad," he said, the admiration obvious in his voice.

Now it was Leah's turn to smirk. She flopped down onto a bench and lifted the bar high above her chest. "Don't let this fall on me with your little girl arms."

Jay stood over her on the spotter position. "Go."

"One. Two. Three. Four." The bar started to get heavy after the fifth bench press.

"Come on. Come on. You have five more to go."

Leah paused in mid-press, studying Jay's face. She'd never noticed the five-o'clock shadow he got under his chin. It, like everything else about him, was exquisitely sexy.

"What?" Jay squinted down at her.

"Dying." Leah averted her eyes and lifted the weight as high as she could. "Eight. Nine. *Ten*."

"Five more. Come on, babe."

"Liar," Leah panted. "Cheat. Jackass."

"Stop yer whining and move! So, uh, did you get to talk to Jennifer today? You guys are in English together, right?"

"Yeah." Leah continued to lift, pretending to be too out of breath to continue the conversation.

"Yeah, you talked to her, or, yeah, you guys are in English together?"

"English together." Leah sat up and lowered the bar. "I think I need a forty for my next set."

"You going to talk to her for me, or do I have to make an ass out of myself in person?" Jay ignored her request and sat down beside her.

"Tomorrow," Leah said, hoping the guilt wasn't

too obvious in her tone. She was a lousy liar. She had no intention of talking to Jennifer tomorrow, the day after or ever about Jay's interest in being her Snow Ball date. And she certainly wasn't going to share with Jay her secret fantasy of losing enough weight to get up enough courage to ask him out herself.

Leah winced as she rubbed her shoulders. She was going to be sore as hell tomorrow. Her workouts would be greatly dwindled until her muscles healed again. "I don't know how I'm ever going to lose all this weight," she muttered, pinching an inch of skin around her waist.

"You'll do it." Jay gently shoved her hand away from the pinching. "Don't push yourself too hard. You're in pretty good shape already, you know."

Not nearly as good as Jennifer. Leah had a vision of Jennifer leaping into the air, pom-poms in hand, hard abs flashing the audience. No, definitely not nearly as good as Jennifer.

"Yeah, right." Leah released his hand. Reluctantly. She loved holding his hand. She would give anything to be able to do it anytime.

"Please. How many jump shots did you make during the game yesterday?"

"A lot." Leah smiled. Two times more than the rest of the team combined. At the rate at which she sank baskets, there was no chance that Sonoma would miss out on the state finals this year. She was bound to get them there single-handedly.

"You're the star out there. Don't stress out too much about this whole weight thing. You'll get there."

"Yeah, I guess so." Leah suddenly couldn't stop smiling.

He smiled back and gently flicked her chin. She held her breath as his hand lingered a bit longer than usual. Their eyes met and Jay parted his lips. "Le—"

"Dalal! Get a room or get on the court!"

Leah's eyes popped open and came face-to-face with a basketball coming full speed toward them. Instinctively, her hands flew into the air and she caught the ball in midair, breathing a sigh of relief. If she came home with a broken nose, her mama would smack her into next week.

"Good catch, babe." Tony Qi, a lithe Chinese senior, gave Jay a knowing grin, glancing at Leah.

Leah blushed. *Babe?*

And what had just almost happened between her and Jay? He'd almost kissed her. Right there in public. In front of everyone.

"Hey." Tony nodded toward Leah. "You must be Jennifer. Sorry for interrupting."

Leah's smile disappeared. No, she certainly was *not*. Apparently Jay had told all his friends about his interest in the petite cheerleader. And apparently he had forgotten to give a physical description.

"Uh, this is Leah, actually." Jay sprang to his feet. "My neighbor. I was helping her get a workout in before you nearly killed us. Nice going."

Neighbor? That was it? That was all she was to him?

"Sorry." Tony shrugged. "You coming or what? Coach was wondering where you were."

"Damn. Sorry, Leah. Practice."

"I get it," Leah said shortly. "I gotta go. I see Coach giving me a dirty look."

"See you out front at six?"

"Fine. Whatever."

Jay didn't even hear her as he took off after Tony, tackling him hard onto the floor of the court. "Jackass!"

Leah watched the boys roughhouse for a few minutes out of the corner of her eye. He'd already forgotten about what had almost taken place between them.

Leah felt a tightening in her stomach and for a second, she thought she was going to bawl right there.

Wuss.

Dumb-ass wuss. Shut the hell up and pull yourself together.

Leah swore to herself not to get that caught up in him again. Obviously, he was flirting with her. But he wasn't going to go any further.

Not yet anyway.

She had to work fast. If Jay was actually telling people about Jennifer, it was getting serious. She could lose him for good if she didn't get up the nerve to actually make a move.

The next morning, Leah lay in bed, actually enjoying the feeling of each muscle twitching painfully. She'd worked hard for each of those twitches and every single sore joint. She closed her eyes, remembering Jay's expression as he drove her home. She'd been polite, but cold. No movie quotes. No ribbing. He'd asked her three times if she was okay.

She didn't need to make it too easy on him. If he could forget her in three seconds, she could do the same to him.

"Leah! Did you want to come to Cardio Bar with me or not?"

Cardio Bar.

A workout catered to skinny-ass chicks. A week ago she would have laughed at Victoria for even suggesting it. Now she would do anything to look like one of those skinny-ass chicks. Even their workout.

"Coming, Mama! Let me get some clothes on." Leah attempted to get up. Pain. Failing that, she fell back onto her bed and gazed out the window at the clear, cloudless sky. Another gorgeous day in L.A. A perfect day for lying around by the pool and working on a glowing tan.

Meoooow. Espresso Bean opened one eye and yawned loudly from the foot of the bed.

"And a great day for playing with kitties. Right, Beanie?"

Meeeeooooow!

"Good girl. Love you, baby." Leah rubbed the cat's tummy and trailed kisses all over her wet, little nose.

Purr.

"You better be wearing something decent, Leah!"

Leah could hear Victoria running around downstairs, pouring coffee and finding her house keys.

"Elle MacPherson comes in there on Saturdays. You want to look like you belong."

Wear something nice for working out?

Wouldn't being sweaty and working out be enough to look as though she belonged?

And who the hell was Elle MacPherson?

This modeling world was insane. She was looking to get in, impress people and get out before she lost her mind as Victoria obviously had.

Leah stepped on the scale clad only in a thin nightshirt. A hundred and ninety-five pounds! *Woo-hoo!*

She was down five pounds already in two days. She

touched her face, the same way Jay had yesterday. She swore she could actually feel her cheekbones through the baby fat today.

She had to keep up the hard work. She was going to lose the weight and twirl in front of Jay and ask him what he thought. *Let's see him say he just wants to be friends then.*

She was going to be the heroine of this story. Not the fat sidekick. That much was certain.

"Leah! You have three minutes to get your sorry butt down here, or I'll—"

"Coming, Mama! Jeez."

Leah scrubbed her teeth and jumped into the first decent workout outfit she could find. A black tracksuit with a racer-back sports bra.

"Bye, Beanie. Sleep. I'll see you in the afternoon." She blew a kiss at the cat.

Leah was pulling her hair into a ponytail when she stopped short on the landing upon seeing Victoria. A low-slung pair of terry-cloth pants. Belly-baring sports bra with rhinestones. A belly chain. Where the hell were they going?

"Baby, don't you think a bit of makeup would—"

"Mama. I am *not* wearing makeup to Cardio Bar!"

"Just hold still."

Before Leah could protest further, Victoria pulled

bronzer out of her gym bag and dusted a puff across Leah's cheekbones and over her nose.

She ducked away before the lip gloss came out.

"When you see the other women, you'll feel sorry," Victoria warned.

Whatever, belly-chain woman. Leah didn't dare say it out loud.

Thirty minutes later, Leah understood what Victoria had meant.

Cardio Bar was dainty step aerobics to cheesy Britney Spears music from the nineties. Not a single bead of sweat or misplaced hair in sight.

Leah pounded through the set routine for the fourth time and yawned. *This* was a challenging cardio workout? She got more of a workout warming up before practice.

Not to mention the instructor. Instead of a hyper-active blond cheerleader type, they'd gotten a David Beckham look-alike who seemed to want to be anywhere but in Cardio Bar.

All the women in the class were in Juicy Couture workout outfits with their hair perfectly pinned up. Most wore earrings. Some wore heavy gemstone necklaces. All wore makeup. A lot of it.

None of them needed to work out. All were perfect size 0s and looked as though they had never seen any size in the positive numbers. Any of them could be a model.

Leah sighed. *Unfair.* They were here for social hour. Those women in the back were just grown-up versions of Jennifer and Shazan. Victoria fit in perfectly with them. Was Leah ever going to get that chance?

Hop over the step. Step back. Hop up one foot. Hop back down on opposite foot. Hop. Hop. Hop.

She felt like a freaking dancing bunny.

She glanced behind to see what Victoria was doing. Chatting up a tall, gorgeous blonde who looked vaguely familiar. Elle McDonald's or whatever probably.

"Darling, you are truly incredible! Are you a model like your mum?"

The sole man in the class, an English gentleman who managed to look the part even in workout gear, was the only one focused on the instructor. And the only one who talked to her.

"No." Leah stopped to sip from her bottle, more from boredom rather than thirst.

"Well, you should be."

"Yeah?" Leah's ears perked up and she glanced down at her stomach. It did seem to be flatter than she'd remembered. Maybe the five pounds she'd lost were showing more than she'd expected.

"Definitely. A few more pounds and wow. That ass

is ready for showtime. You probably just have what, twenty, thirty more pounds to go?"

Leah rolled her eyes. Only in L.A. could people randomly comment on your weight as if you were a piece of steak.

"Why?" Leah gave him a dirty look. "You gotta problem with that?"

Wannabe David Beckham changed the music to an Enya song. Instantly, the class dropped onto the mats into yoga poses. Victoria was still glued to the McDonald's lady's side.

Leah lowered herself into the floor, wishing she could disappear. This was such a waste of time.

"Don't get huffy! I'm just giving you the same advice I give all my clients." The annoying twerp leaned over his bent knees and breathed loudly.

"Clients?"

"I'm a life coach."

"A what?" Leah stayed sitting up. Whatever the hell everyone else was doing, she wanted no part in it. Weird om-shanti stuff. She'd wanted a workout and obviously this wasn't the place for it.

"Life coach. Coach for life."

"I get it."

"When girls come to me, fat, sad, miserable, I tell them, go online. Look at Web sites of girls who look the way you want to. Emulate them. Be them."

"Be them?" Leah started to laugh. "Kidnap them, peel off their skin and tape it to yourself?"

"Ew!"

"You said it."

"Trust me, love. Look up 'thinspiration.' You'll see the kind of woman you want to be."

Thinspiration, huh? Leah stored that nugget of information away.

"You won't believe the girls I've coached. Did you know a certain rich socialite who's recently lost close to twenty-five pounds? She's finally in the single digits."

"Single digits?"

"Under the magic hundred."

"What?"

"You know, the magic hundred. Under a hundred pounds. Doors open for you, love. You get invited to parties, the boys love you, people know you."

"A hundred pounds? That's like a big dog. Or a big kid. Is that normal?"

"Completely. Remember, no one likes a fat girl." With that he dropped into a sleeping pose. "Ommmm…"

No one likes a fat girl.

How true.

four

The Devil Wears Prada
178 lbs

"YOU look good, little girl." Victoria stood on one foot in the doorway of Leah's room, slipping on a teetering pair of wraparound stilettos. "I don't know what you've been doing, but it's worked for you. Perfect."

Leah sucked in her abs. Perfect? Still not quite yet. But better. Definitely much better. It had been a torturous two weeks of eating extremely well along with three-hour workouts per day. But it had been worth it. Twenty-two whole pounds had dropped off and every part of her body felt tighter and more toned. Just in time for the *Jade* magazine benefit.

She'd become practically a recluse during her

rigorous diet and exercise regime, shunning ice-cream socials or even riding to and from school with Jay. She didn't want anyone to know how hard she was working. How every pound was pure torture.

She'd walked the three miles from home to school every day. As soon as classes were over, she ran three to four miles on the treadmill, lifted weights and then focused on basketball practice.

And the food. She'd shunned all bread and pasta. And ice cream. Only protein shakes, salad and deli meat. But it had been worth it. The pounds had melted off and she saw a drastic drop in her weight every single morning.

And she'd been wearing oversize T-shirts and baggy sweatpants so no one would be able to see her progress. Not even herself.

Now as she stood in front of the first full-length mirror she'd allowed in her room, Leah was surprised by how good her body looked in the cobalt-blue A-line dress. A few weeks ago, she never would have dreamed of wearing anything so formfitting, let alone sleeveless.

A navy pashmina draped around her arms hid the remaining upper arm flab she was having the hardest time getting rid of. Still a lot of work to do till she looked anywhere close to Shazan or Jenn.

"You're ready, girl." Her mother finished adjusting her shoes and hair. As predicted, Victoria was a vision in a champagne-pink dress. She glowed like an illuminated oil lamp. "No one will be able to take their eyes off you tonight."

Leah smiled at Victoria, who had spent an hour doing her makeup for her. Eyeliner, blush, lipstick, bronzer. The works. They'd really been getting along the past two weeks with Victoria treating her as almost an equal. Finally, Leah'd felt like her mother's daughter, for the first time realizing how fantastic it was to feel almost...pretty. She gave her head a little shake to watch Victoria's sapphire earrings dance in the lamplight. This whole makeup and jewelry thing was working out pretty well for her. She hoped the night would be as magical as Victoria wanted it to be.

"Ready."

Leah's nerves were quiet during the drive to the NELL where the gala was being held. Unfortunately, as soon as she stepped out of the car, her legs started to tremble and shake. She shivered even though the night air was muggy.

God, all those people were going to be judging her tonight. Was she ready for that? What if she didn't look nearly as good as she thought she did? What if they pointed and demanded to know what the "plus-size girl" was doing there?

She needed to get out of here. She fingered her cell phone in her purse. She could call Jay, beg him to come get her. The last thing she wanted to do was ruin Victoria's reputation by looking out of place.

"Come on." Victoria turned back to gaze at Leah. "Girl, you're gorgeous. I promise you! Or you wouldn't be here!"

Victoria wouldn't say it if she didn't mean it. Not in the course of her entire life had Victoria ever called Leah "gorgeous."

Leah smiled weakly at her mother. "Coming, coming."

No, she couldn't ditch this thing. She'd worked so hard the past two weeks and she had to know if it had been worth it or not.

A warm rush of air greeted Leah as she and Victoria stepped inside the heavy doors of the NELL. In the distance, she could hear the sounds of the band playing "Moon River" over a din of laughter and glasses clinking.

God, she hated these things.

"Victoria." Alfreddo Riviera, Botoxed, tanned and wrinkle-free in a refrigerator-white suit, materialized by her mother's side within seconds of Victoria and Leah checking in their coats.

"Hello, darling," Victoria murmured, brushing the air near each of Alfreddo's cheeks with her lips, her right hand grazing his shoulder. "You remember Lynnette, of course."

"Ah, of course. Lynnette." His eyes skimmed her from eyeballs to toes so quickly Leah barely had a chance to blink before he was done. Leah fought back the urge to smirk as Alfreddo raised his eyebrows. "You're looking...quite marvelous. Have you been away on holiday?"

Yeah, sure. Hell of a holiday.

Before she could say a word, Victoria cut in. "Yes, she is. She's a shoo-in for the Daughters segment. She's a foot taller than these other little girls! At least!"

Ugh. The magazine spread. Leah'd almost forgotten the whole point of this stupid gala. As an "audition" for which mother-daughter pairs were going to be chosen for the Mother's Day special.

"I know never to doubt you again, darling. You said she'd be ready and she is." Alfreddo took Victoria's arm and gently brushed her cheek with his mouth. He then paused to turn back to Leah. "Not that I ever doubted you, my dear."

Leah gritted her teeth. What had Victoria told him? "Plus-size modeling, my ass," she muttered under her breath. Sleazy Alfreddo didn't even have the decency to look even slightly embarrassed.

"Come along, both of you. I must introduce you to Anne LeFleur. She will be making the final decisions on the mother-daughter pairs tonight. She'll be choosing four pairs out of all of these agencies."

Oh, goody. Let the horse auction begin.

Leah watched Alfreddo lead Victoria across the room, his arm settled comfortably around her waist. That man hadn't let go of her for even an instant. Leah had always assumed Alfreddo was gay, but after the way his fingers were trailing freely around Victoria's minuscule hips, Leah was certain this was not the case. She reluctantly followed. There was no way she was leaving her mother alone with that creep.

Leah stopped a few feet away from the *Jade* people; two trailing assistants hovered around an imposing woman in a strapless white gown who did the cheek-kiss thing with both Alfreddo and Victoria. The woman's fire-colored hair was piled atop her head and her almond-shaped eyes scrutinized everyone carefully, all the while the serene smile never leaving her face. The whole scene reminded Leah of *The Devil Wears Prada*.

All the fake kissing and the whispered murmuring made Leah feel like more of an outsider than ever. She had no idea what anyone was talking about. Or what to do with her hands. She wished her dress had pockets for her to stick them into.

All the gushing about whether Prada made the gown or Calvin Klein. Whether Oribe did someone's hair or Rita Hazan was making her slightly nauseated. What she could really use was a goblet of champagne and an hors d'oeuvre to calm her nerves.

Speaking of food, where *was* it? Leah looked around. Band. Check. Tables for cliquey mingling. Check. Ah, the spread. The table started with raw vegetables, dip and other healthy stuff and ended with a ham. A scrumptious, juicy ham that two servers were slivering pieces off of.

Leah's mouth watered. To ensure a flat stomach for tonight, she had eaten practically nothing. Two baby tangerines six hours apart. That had been it.

"Lynnette Mandeville."

Leah nearly jumped. The red-haired woman was inches away from her face.

"Yes, ma'am," Leah said, feeling as though she should curtsy or something.

"Anne LeFleur. The pleasure is all mine."

"Oh! Not at all. It's—" Leah practically gagged. Anne was wearing an entire bottle of Poison perfume. The heavy floral scent infiltrated Leah's nose. She could feel an instant headache starting on the back of her neck.

"My, you are tall. And what lovely skin." The woman reached out and gently grazed Leah's cheek with her fingertips. "You are your mother's daughter."

"Thanks," Leah gasped. Air. She needed air.

The woman abruptly turned to face Alfreddo, swishing yet another gust of perfume in Leah's face. "She'll need to fit into the sample sizes. Will that be possible?"

"Ahmm." Leah bit her lip to keep from gagging out loud, not caring that she was licking off her burgundy lipstick. What the heck were sample sizes? And why were all these people talking about her to Alfreddo?

"Anne, darling, you have nothing to worry about. This is only an intermediate phase Lynnette is going through. She will be absolutely prepared." Alfreddo nuzzled Victoria's neck. "What do you say, darling?"

Darling?

Leah started. "I had a question about sample siz—"

"Lynnette and Victoria. Duo number two." Anne snapped her fingers at assistant number one, who was frantically writing something in a notebook. "But please have a backup pair ready, Alfreddo, pet. We can't afford to have any...*mishaps* on the day of the shoot. Demi and Tallulah don't have that kind of time."

"There will be no mishaps, am I right, Lynnette?" Alfreddo the pet practically purred, turning his eyes to Leah, expression not changing. The man's face never moved with all the collagen pumped into his skin.

Leah's head swung back and forth as if she were

watching a Ping-Pong tournament. Before she could get around to understanding what the heck was going on, Anne LeFleur and her cronies were swept away, the trains of their gowns leaving Leah, Victoria and Alfreddo in the dust.

"Um, what is a sample size?" Leah was the first to speak up. "What is it that I need to fit into?"

A smile broke out across Victoria's face. "We did it. We're in. It's going to happen."

"Um, awesome. But what the hell is a sample size, Mama?"

"Size 0 or a 2," Alfreddo helpfully filled in.

"Oh." The headache was getting worse.

"You'll get there, little girl. You keep eating healthy and working out, you'll be there in no time. You still got two months to drop this baby fat." Victoria glowed. "I can't believe how simple that was. Alfreddo, baby, you are a miracle worker." With that Victoria planted a big smooch on Alfreddo's lips.

He kissed her back.

No way. That was even too disgusting to think about.

Leah turned away and haltingly took a seat at the nearest table. Size 0 or 2. That was at least thirty more pounds. More like forty. She was suddenly filled with a deep emptiness. For once it didn't feel like hunger.

* * *

A low whistle greeted Leah as she and Victoria arrived home.

"First you ignore me, then you replace my best friend with this total babe?" The basketball Jay had been dribbling thudded to the ground as Leah closed the passenger-side door of Victoria's Viper.

Leah raised an eyebrow. Did he just call her a total babe? "What do you want?"

"Uh-huh. No ignoring the question. What gives?" Jay's voice dripped with feigned indignation as he stepped over the waist-high shrub that separated their properties.

"I'm going to bed." Victoria patted Leah on the cheek. "Don't stay out too late. You need your beauty sleep. Good night, Jay."

"I won't," Leah said at the same time as Jay said, "Good night, Ms. Mandeville."

Leah waited till Victoria was safely inside the front door before turning to Jay. "I'm not ignoring you, jackass."

"So what gives? What's all this?" Jay gestured toward her coiffed hair and shimmering dress. "Did you go to that modeling thing?"

She motioned him to take a seat on the steps of her front porch. Her heeled feet had gone numb over half an hour ago while Alfreddo had dragged her from entertainment agent to photographer back to agent, introducing her as the "new face of the industry."

"Yeah, I did. It was pretty cool, actually. Not nearly as horrible as last time."

"Oh, yeah?"

"Yeah. I'm going to do a photo shoot in a few months. The magazine people liked me. Some Mother's Day thing with Hollywood types."

Leah smiled remembering Anne LeFleur touching her cheek. As she'd found out later, impressing the woman was not an easy feat. Apparently, she had a reputation for glancing disdainfully at new models and telling them to pick another profession because "thissss one is *cccccertainly* not for *youuuuu*."

"Quite a day for you, huh? First, you regulated West Hollywood's ass in the game and then you get a whole modeling gig. Cool."

"That's me. So hot I'm cool." Leah flashed back to the game. She'd been freezing on the court and kept her warm-ups on the whole time. But her game was still on and at the end the score was 25–3.

"Well, you look hot. I can't believe how much weight you've lost."

"Thanks."

"How much weight *have* you lost, by the way? I hope you're not crash-dieting."

"I still have a lot more to go." Leah ignored the

question and rested her elbows on her knees. "At least thirty pounds."

Jay frowned. "You look great the way you are. I mean..." He followed the hem of her skirt as it rode up her legs. "Better than great. I've never seen you like this before."

The words she'd been waiting for. She tilted her head toward his and she could swear Jay scooted a tad closer to her as he gave her a shoulder bump.

Leah got up enough courage to lightly squeeze his hand. "Oh, yeah? Thanks."

"'And a tip of the cap to you, Miss Corningstone.'"

Ugh. He almost never caught her off guard. Which movie was that from? Her brain seemed to be in sluggish mode after the party. Or from the lack of food. She was proud that she hadn't touched a bite of food or champagne, despite Alfreddo's insistence she do a toast with Victoria and him to her success. She'd toasted, pretended to take a sip, then put the glass down. Net calories for the day? Around a hundred.

"Hint."

"Miss Corningstone equals Christina Applegate. One of the most perfect women on the—"

"*Anchorman*. Damn. That one was easy."

Jay laughed. "You're allowed to miss a shot every once in a while. But don't make a habit out of it."

"How can I with you around?"

Jay laughed and they sat in silence for a few minutes, hands lightly touching. Leah's breathing remained steady and deep, despite her heart thudding wildly. She was practically holding hands with Jay. And he'd initiated it.

Jay cleared his throat. "Ride with me to school tomorrow?"

Leah gave what she hoped was a confident laugh, "Wouldn't miss it, *babe*."

Jay laughed, Leah thought, nervously.

After a few more minutes of nervous chatter, Leah managed to say good-night. The second she was in her bedroom, she stripped out of the dress and stepped on the scale.

A hundred and seventy-four pounds.

Not eating the whole day had worked. That was twenty-six pounds total so far. She could do this. She had two months to lose all her baby fat and fit into a size 0. She could do it. How many pounds was that? Forty? Thirty-five? A hundred?

Too many.

Her head whirled at the thought. Leah sat heavily on the bed and rested her head between her knees. The dizziness had come and gone all week, but it was never this bad. She should eat something.

No. Tomorrow. She would eat tomorrow. Just

enough to keep her energy up. But tonight she would go to bed with the memories of Jay's eyes skimming her body and the promise of good things to come.

five

Run, Lola, Run
170 lbs

"YOU look so good!" Shazan exclaimed as Leah pried open her locker, freshly showered and dressed after practice. "Everyone's talking about it!"

"Thanks." Leah smiled. This was not the first time she had gotten that exact compliment that day. At least six people had commented on her new look, Shazan being the latest.

"God, look at your waist! It's so teeny-tiny!"

"Yeah, right." Leah couldn't help the pride in her voice. After all the good things Jay had said over the weekend, she couldn't help but show off her new figure at school on Monday. None of her old clothes fit and she had to resort to borrowing one of her mom's old Diane von Furstenberg wrap dresses. It was almost cheating in slimming navy with white diagonal pinstripes, but she didn't care.

"You've been dieting, right? We haven't seen you at lunch in weeks."

"I've lost about twenty pounds." Leah lowered her eyes modestly. Closer to thirty actually, but no one needed to know that.

Shazan frowned. "Wow. That's a lot. How many weeks have you been dieting?"

Leah slowly opened her purse and pulled out a ChapStick. Her lips were constantly chapped. They were bleeding in the middle of class that day. "A little over two."

"Two weeks? Wow! I thought it was supposed to be, like, two to five pounds a week or something. Ten pounds a week is kinda fast, right? What have you been doing?"

Leah glanced down at her reflection in the mirror. Considering the fact that she was down to a piece of dry wheat toast for breakfast, a salad for lunch, some almonds for a snack and a piece of grilled chicken with, again, miserable salad for dinner… no, it was not at all fast. In fact, it was slow, painful torture. Even being around food drove her nuts and she had taken to eating lunch quickly in the locker room and sneaking in a jog on the treadmill.

"I guess it's mostly water weight. You know, quick weight loss and stuff," Leah fibbed quickly. She was a terrible liar and Shazan would never fall for it.

"Yeah, I do know. God, I wish I could lose thirty pounds. I'm *sooo* jealous. Those pills of mine help, though. You want any?"

Leah glanced at Shazan's already protruding collarbone. Thirty pounds less and she'd die. "If they're working for you, why the hell not?"

"Sure, just let me know. I order them online from Mexico. My mom would freak out if she found out." Shazan rolled her eyes. "Hey, Jenn!"

Leah cursed under her breath. Jennifer Chan, her archnemesis. And her day had been going so well.

"Hey, girlies!" Jennifer tossed her ebony hair, her miniskirt swishing as she strutted toward them. "Leah, you okay? I didn't know if you'd go to practice today after what happened in geometry."

"What happened?" Shazan glanced from Jennifer to Leah. "You okay?"

Argh. Of course Jennifer would have to bring that up. As if she actually cared. Annoying little bitch.

"I'm fine, I'm fine. Just needed to lie down, that's all." Leah slammed her locker shut after grabbing her backpack, stuffed full of books waiting to be read for homework.

The topic of the day in geometry had been obtuse angles, which Leah knew nothing about because she'd skipped class the week before to lift weights.

Mr. Roberts's voice had practically lulled Leah to sleep, so when he had called on her to put a problem on the board, she'd struggled for a few minutes scribbling this and that until the teacher had to give her a hint. A big hint, but still, she had figured it out on her own.

But that wasn't all. It was the dizzy spell she had suffered midproblem that had prompted Mr. Roberts to ask her if she wanted to see the school nurse. Leah, not wanting to waste a golden opportunity, had practically skipped out of class and run to the gym for some free throws before that afternoon's practice.

"I'm fine. I, uh, ate something weird for lunch."

"Sushi?"

"Salad. It probably had bad lettuce."

"Hey, Leah. Did you notice that huge bruise on your shoulder?" Shazan lifted the sleeve of Leah's dress. "Looks pretty painful. Where did you get this?"

Leah touched the tender spot. "I don't know. Must have been practice. I didn't even feel it."

Both girls gazed at her with worried looks.

"If you say so." Jennifer still looked doubtful.

"Hey! Let's go shopping next weekend." Shazan finished applying a coat of lipstick and took a swig of bottled water followed by two of her handy diet pills. "I need to get my Snow Ball dress."

Leah watched Jennifer closely. Had Jay asked her? Maybe, just maybe, he had decided not to.

"Not me. I still don't know if I'm going." Jennifer shrugged ruefully. "No one's asked yet."

Yes!

"I gotta meet Jay. He's giving me a ride," Leah announced loftily as she tossed her backpack over her shoulder. "See you guys later, okay?"

"Call me later!" Shazan called behind her.

"Sure thing," Leah called back, feeling a warmth pooling through her. It was already happening. Even losing a few pounds had the pretty girls wanting to go shopping with her.

Jennifer followed Leah as she wove through the postbell crowd to get to the parking lot.

"You do look great, Leah. I heard you're doing a modeling thing with your mom?"

"Yeah. For *Jade* magazine." Leah tried to walk faster. Why was Jennifer following her?

"Wow. My mom makes dumplings all day. It must be so glamorous," Jennifer sighed. "All those famous people."

"Yeah, it is. There are always tons of really good-looking photographers around. And the clothes she brings home! They're really amazing. We're going to get to meet some pretty famous people at this shoot. Goldie and Kate and all those people." Leah couldn't help but rub it in. Jennifer always had it all. It was nice to have the upper hand for once.

As Leah and Jennifer exited the doors of the school, Leah spotted Jay high-fiving Tony Qi and Jason Jones next to the Mustang. As she approached, his eyes lit up.

"There she is. I've been looking for you all day. Did you get my e-mail?"

Leah opened her mouth to ask, "What e-mail?" but before she could, Jennifer practically shoved her aside and was by Jay's side in an instant.

"So what did you want to ask me?" she practically purred. Jay's friends hooted and punched each other's shoulders.

Jay grinned and suddenly Leah's heart stopped beating. "Will you be my date for the Snow Ball or what? How many hints do I have to drop?"

Leah lay facedown on the floor of her room, panting. Her white T-shirt was officially see-through from the half gallon of sweat that had leaked from her pores. Thank God for the padded sports bra she wore underneath that kept her from giving a peep show to half of Hollywood Hills.

"Arrr…"

Eight miles. That was the farthest she had run in her entire life. It was amazing what anger and hurt could drive a person to do. Instead of riding home with Jay, she'd made a lame excuse and run the hell away from the nauseous scene of him and Jennifer making googly eyes at each other. She couldn't face him. Not now. Not after her expression had obviously given away her shock, then hurt, then anger. His friends had seen. Everyone had seen. She had jogged the five miles around the track and then run home, ten-pound pack on her back.

She was dying and didn't know which pain was worse. Physical, or the heavy rock where her heartache was supposed to be.

"Ahh!" The cramp that had attacked her thigh around mile three still hadn't let up. *"Damn!"*

She writhed in pain on the floor, putting pressure on the cramp till the twitching subsided. Maybe the physical pain was worse. For now anyway.

She raised herself onto one elbow and pried her eyes open. The room was still spinning. She'd been starving before her workout, but now the growling of her stomach had given way to a hollow rut. Leah touched her lower belly. The pouch of fat was still there. What would it take to get rid of it?

Leah's breathing slowed after a few minutes and she managed to pull herself into a sitting position. Her evening was just beginning. She had loads of homework for geometry, a short story to read for English and a rough draft of an essay due for creative writing.

Plus, she wanted to do the *Absolute Abs* DVD she'd found in her mother's endless exercise DVD collection. The pouch would be gone by the end of the day. She was sure of it.

But first, she would check her weight. Seeing those numbers drop every day always put her into a good mood. If there was any chance of a good mood after the day's events. She couldn't believe Jay had sucker punched her like that.

Leah stepped onto the scale and waited.

One-seventy.

How was that even possible? Leah stepped off the scale and back on again after she'd shucked off her sweaty workout clothes.

Still one-seventy.

She'd burned off at least a thousand calories that day alone. And she'd eaten only around five hundred calories. And the scale hadn't budged.

"Damn!"

This was insane. What was wrong with her body? She kicked the scale. It had to be broken. She would check at school tomorrow.

Her mood foul, Leah logged in to her e-mail account and scowled when she saw Jay had signed her up for Movie Quote of the Day e-mails. That's all she was good for. His damn movie quotes.

After responding to e-mail from her cousins in Atlanta, Leah started surfing the Web. "Weight Loss Tips," she typed into the Windows Live Web search engine.

Work out. Eat less. Low-Carb.

She knew all this.

She remembered the guy at Cardio Bar. The life coach. What had he said to look up?

"Thinspiration," she typed.

The ancient Dell whirred. If she and her mother did do a kick-ass job at the modeling shoot, she would insist they buy a new computer. One made that decade preferably.

"My friend Ana helped me lose 50 pounds!" an ad on the side of the search results window screamed.

Ana, huh? Leah clicked the link and blinked when she realized what she was seeing.

Thinspiration. Pro-Anorexia. My friend Ana.

"'This site is a pro-Ana Web site and anorexic chat room. It is for support of those who already have anorexia and/or those that accept people that are anorexic or bulimic,'" Leah read out loud. "'Ana is our friend. She is a lifestyle choice that we are willing to make.'"

Ana? Like a person? A *friend*?

These girls were insane. Accepting anorexia as a lifestyle choice? It was a disease. Leah wanted to be thin, but she wasn't that desperate. She'd seen the after-school specials and her mother had told her a fair share of scary anorexic-model stories.

No way.

Leah was about to leave the page and relegate it to her list of crazy-people sites when something on the lower right corner caught her eye. *Thoughts*.

I seem to have reached a plateau. I restrict quite heavily and drink lots of water. I used to be able to lose like that! But now the scale is stationary. Is there any advice out there? Should I up the green tea, or perhaps green tea pills? Or perhaps a liquid fast? Thanks, everyone, for all your support—Fat-Ass.

It was like the poster, Fat-Ass, was reading her mind. Leah eagerly scrolled down to see who had responded.

Try this diet. Leah kept reading. Watermelons. Eat only watermelon for an entire week! Guarantee it'll knock off ten pounds before you know it! Plus, you can eat all the watermelon you want! Extremely low calorie!

Ten pounds! That was two more than what she was hoping to lose in the next week. No doubt that would get rid of her lower-belly pouch. Plus, she loved watermelon.

Leah gazed at the pictures of the poster, Fat-Ass.

The girl certainly was no fat ass. She looked like a model. The kind of model Leah wanted to be at the *Jade* photo shoot. She wasn't gaunt or sickly as Leah had expected anorexics to look.

Sign up here to join our forum.

Why not? Leah decided as she clicked the link. If the advice was good, she would take it. If it was stupid, she would ignore it. In the meantime, watermelon diet it was.

SIX

Watermelon
165 lbs

Leah stared longingly at the side salad Shazan picked at as the two girls ate lunch at Riverside Mall on Friday afternoon. Salad had never looked so good. Her mood was still foul from what had happened at school.

Jay asked that skinny bitch right in front of her! He knew how much it would hurt her and he *still did it!* Jackass! She caught a glimpse of him that morning getting into his Mustang. It wasn't just her imagination; he had definitely glanced at her bedroom window before squealing out of the driveway. He knew.

Her reaction must have totally given her away.

Today she'd been in no mood to sit through an

hour of geometry. Staring at the back of Jennifer's silky black hair. Wishing for the universe to pull a *Freaky Friday* and switch her body with the tiny junior's. Then *she* would be the one kissing Jay by his Mustang for all the school to see.

Luckily, Shazan had insisted Leah cut class and hit the mall for some good old-fashioned retail therapy to celebrate her slim new body.

Not slim enough for Jay, though.

"I need a dress that says, 'I'm sexy, but not a slut,' you know what I mean?" *Whack, whack, whack,* went Shazan's fork. She speared a piece of carrot, then set down the fork without taking a bite of the mouthwatering sliver of orange. "It's going to be mine and Bill's six-month anniversary, so I want the night to be really special."

"Huh." Leah rested her chin on her now-empty water glass.

"What about you? Who are you gonna go with?"

"I don't know." Leah was too busy watching Shazan's fork. "Maybe one of the guys on the team."

"Don't worry, Li. We'll find someone for you. Someone tall. And hot. He has to be hot."

Already found him.

Leah felt a twinge of sadness. How stupid she'd been to think that just because Jay had complimented her on her weight loss, he'd be interested in her as a girl.

She was just another buddy.

She had to just come out and tell him how she felt. She couldn't keep it inside anymore. As soon as possible. In her dreams, he would confess that he felt the same way and had only asked Jennifer out because he didn't think Leah was at all interested in him *that* way.

"I want Bill to want more." Shazan was still talking. "But not so much that he goes and gets it somewhere else."

Leah laughed. "And where would that be, Shazan?"

Bill Collins was good-looking, sweet and, above all, smart. He wasn't about to cheat on one of the hottest girls in school with some random chick who was ready to put out. How could beautiful girls like Shazan be so insecure? If Leah looked anything like her, she would never question herself.

"Oh, there are a lot of possibilities, Leahie." Shazan wrinkled her pert nose, the diamond in her right nostril glinting in the fluorescent lighting. "Those goth junk sluts. Emo-types, you know? They'd screw anyone."

Leah rolled her eyes. "I don't think you need to worry about people who believe they can levitate or turn each other into vampires."

"I know this, and you know this. But...men! You never know what they want, right?"

"That's true." Leah was the last person who was going to claim she knew how the average man's mind worked. She barely even understood the brain of her so-called best friend. He loved Leah for her mind, but Jennifer for her body.

Freaking weird.

"I'm done," Shazan announced as she dropped her fork, pushing back her tray. More than half the salad remained.

"Me, too." Leah looked down at her empty watermelon container. She'd felt like a loser toting a container of watermelon to the mall, but she wasn't about to go off her diet. Especially not for a shopping trip for a dress for a dance she had no date for.

She scraped the sides of the container with her fork. An entire chunk of watermelon gone, just like that. She felt full of water, yet her stomach still growled angrily.

The diet was working. This morning, three days of watermelon and only watermelon later, she was five pounds lighter.

Her stomach gurgled, loudly enough that Shazan looked up from where she was rummaging in her purse. "You sure you're done? Your stomach seems to be sayin' something else."

Leah laughed, realizing how hollow her voice sounded. "The first thirty weren't bad, but now...I can't stop feeling hungry all the time. I don't know how you can just get by on salads alone. I've never seen you eat anything else."

Shazan plunked down her pill bottle. "I'm telling you. These work."

Leah scrutinized the clear bottle, half-full with shimmery pink pills. *EZ Loze. Fills your stomach so you don't feel hungry! Includes caffeine to give you just enough of an energy boost!*

Leah sighed. She hated the idea of popping pills. It just felt so...addictive.

But as she watched Shazan take a swallow of water followed by two of the pills, she couldn't help but marvel at Shazan's tiny waist and defined cheekbones.

Shazan had a boyfriend who was crazy about her. She had tons of friends and always fit in anywhere she went. She could slip on any outfit in the whole mall and have it look fantastic on her. Leah wanted all that. One of the coolest girls at school did this stuff, Leah argued with herself. *Why not me?* "Okay, gimme. A few please. I need to get through the rest of this day without eating everything in sight."

Shazan looked amused as Leah carefully popped one pill and tucked the other five away into the pockets of her oversize cargo pants. "Fine. But make sure you eat before the game tomorrow, okay? You look great now, and we're all proud of you, but if you lose this game, I'll personally kick your ass."

Leah playfully punched Shazan in the shoulder. "Don't worry your pretty little head, girl. I know what I'm doing. I'm not going to screw our only chance at the finals."

The girls cleared away their trays and Leah shoved her empty watermelon container into her leather bag. She'd never carried a purse in her life, but the hot-pink crocodile tote had been her first purchase of the day. Shazan had insisted the purse was "so her."

How could Leah argue with something that was "so her"? The modeling gig better pay well, though. She'd paid more for the purse than her wardrobe for a year. "I need a bathing suit, too. Mama's dragging me to L.A. next weekend for some modeling shoot."

"Lucky."

"Yeah, have you seen my stomach?" Leah patted her lower belly. Definitely better, but still not flat.

"Whatever. Take those pills. By next weekend, you'll be a stick."

"More like a tree stump."

"No more negativity!"

Negativity? It was the truth!

Leah suddenly missed Jay. His friendship. His one-liners. He would be making fun of the whole situation with her by now. Instead, she wanted to be a "girl" and had to act like it.

"Come on, let's go to Forever 21. They always have the cutest dresses around this time." Shazan led the way into the clear-glass store with mannequins wearing sheer, slouchy clothes in the window. Leah had always walked by and glanced in curiously, but had always felt too self-conscious of going in. Seemed that only skinny Asian women frequented the store.

"Ahh, I don't know about this," Leah muttered as Shazan smiled at the greeter and headed toward the back of the store. "Isn't everything a bit... sparkly in here?"

"Oh my God, strapless is totally back!" Shazan ignored Leah and fingered a slinky, fitted dress.

"Oh, goody. Bra fat."

"Shut up, Leah! God. This is adorable! You have to try it on."

"Hell, no!"

"Look at this!"

"Uh, Shaz—"

"Look. You need a dress. Now just do what I say!"

Within twenty minutes, Leah's arms were piled high with shimmery, floaty dresses, eyes rolling toward the ceiling. Shazan had a similar pile.

"You're so lucky the dressing-room line is short today. Come on!"

The girls got rooms next door to each other and both pulled the curtains closed.

Leah tried on the first dress, a shimmery black straight up-and-down number. It highlighted her newly toned arms nicely, but the narrow, straight cut seemed to make her hips even wider. Leah frowned. Pass.

"Let me see!" Shazan's singsong voice was insistent.

Leah shyly pushed back the curtain and noticed Shazan was wearing a similar dress but in a snowy white. She looked like a goddess with her chocolatey curls piled atop her head.

"Hmm…" Shazan frowned.

Leah could practically hear her thoughts. *The dress is cute, too bad her butt's so damn big.*

"Try the pink one. I think the flare will balance you out more."

Leah practically tore the skinny dress off, the tight fabric suffocating her. God, she hated this. How could she have felt so confident and beautiful the night of the benefit? She had had so much more to lose.

She slipped on the "pink one," a strapless lavender dress with a ballerina skirt. She couldn't even get the dress zipped up the back, and the flimsy skirt made her legs look like wooden blocks.

Tears welled in her eyes as she pried the dress off.

"Leah?"

"One sec."

The next dress, a pale green one-shoulder thing, wouldn't even fit around her thighs.

"I think I need a bigger size. For all of these." Leah heard the dejection in her own voice.

"Oh." Leah could hear Shazan's tone change. "Really? Let me see what I can find."

Leah sat on the floor of the dressing room, wiping at the tears on her cheeks. She was a mess. What had she been thinking? Sitting in geometry staring at Jennifer's head was better than this torture.

"Hey." Shazan slid a pile of satin and lace through the curtain. "I got all the larges I could find. Try these on. I know one of them will fit you."

One of them. That was her. The largest of the large.

Leah finally settled on a corseted red dress with a halter neck and a flared skirt in the largest size the store carried. She slowly exited the dressing room, wishing she had come alone. Why did she bring someone to witness her humiliation? And Shazan of all people. Perfect Shazan.

Shazan, meanwhile, had purchased half the store. Leah watched enviously as her friend threw one tiny top after another onto the cashier's table, followed by the white goddess dress.

Not fair.

As the cashier rang up the purchases, Shazan turned to Leah. "Did you hear about Jennifer and Jay?"

"Yeah." Leah busied herself by sifting through her bag for a tube of lip gloss. "He asked her to the ball."

Shazan giggled, dark eyes flashing. "And that's not all! She really likes him a lot. So much that she's considering asking him to get a room at the hotel for afterward. Can you believe that? Miss Goody Two-shoes herself!"

Leah froze. Jennifer and Jay having sex? If that happened, all of this was for nothing.

Suddenly Leah felt very nauseated. She couldn't lose him. He was the one stable force in her life. She had to lose this weight, she had to look fabulous at the dance. She had to get him. No matter what.

"Hey, Shaz. Could I get a few more of those pills?"

seven

She's All That
159 lbs

"Leah, could you please move a bit to the left, me love? You're blockin' the light," Cillian, the photographer's assistant, shielded his eyes and called in his heavy Irish accent. "Roald needs to get one last shot. Then I'm all yours," he said in a much softer voice.

"My bad." Leah ducked to the left, trying not to laugh, and nearly toppled into a sand dune. She'd been stupid to wear three-inch heels at the beach, but all the other models were doing it. "Sorry about your light. Can I make it better?"

"I'll haveta show ya how later, love," he replied,

glancing over to see if his boss could hear them. Apparently he could, from the smirk on his lips.

That was the third time she'd blocked the photographer's light. The first time was when she'd snuck up to see if Cillian was as hot up close as he was from a distance.

He was.

The second time was pretty much for the same reason. Except he had most definitely noticed what she was up to and had made sure to check her out, too, head to toe, with a very apparent smirk.

Amazing what a pink leopard-printed bikini, perfect blowout, and a see-through sarong could do for an otherwise ordinary girl.

"Leah, you better be paying attention!" Victoria called from where she was perched on a beach chair, her golden skin glistening from the half bottle of baby oil and shimmer powder the makeup artist had sprayed her with. "Come closer and see how the light works."

"Don't go far." Cillian took his eyes off the models and winked at her. "I'm not close to done with you yet."

Tan, Irish and eighteen, Cillian had worked for Roald and Alfreddo for about a month. From the way he'd been flirting with her, she guessed this wasn't the first time he'd help shoot models.

"You've had plenty of chances," Leah flirted back. He'd been taking pictures of her with his own camera in between breaks and making suggestive comments all afternoon. In turn, she'd been very dramatically spreading out a beach towel, applying sunblock, pulling her shades over her eyes and pretending to gaze into the distance while leaning back on her elbows. All the while, she'd kept a pouty-lipped, "half eyes closed" expression on her face. All tricks she'd picked up from the Brazilian bombshells down by the waterfront.

The crew had at least ten lights trained on the small group of models lounging on towels, under umbrellas and on beach chairs while makeup artists stood by breathlessly, powder puffs ready to do their thing in between shots. Out-of-date hip-hop music blasting from a centralized iPod assured the modeling staff that they were still young and cool.

"Enjoying yourself?"

Leah recognized Alfreddo by his perfectly pedicured toenails.

"Yeah." She verified her sarong was still knotted around her waist before glancing over at him. She was comfortable revealing her body in front of Cillian's admiring eyes. Alfreddo just gave her a creepy feeling, like dribbling ice-cold oil down her back.

He plunked down a six-pack of beer and a tub of sunblock and, uninvited, took a seat next to her on the dune. "What an amazing view," he said as he uncapped a light beer, his Bermuda shorts riding up his legs to almost a vulgar point. "That'll be you pretty soon, babe. Lights, camera, action. The whole shebang."

The whole shebang? People still said *shebang*? Leah rolled her eyes. She hated when old people tried to use phrases they thought were cool. Groovy, foxy and, worse yet, *jiggy*.

Ugh.

"I bet."

Alfreddo liberally applied robin's egg–blue sunblock to his legs. "You're lucky. You never have to worry about looking washed out or pale in winter."

God, he was like a girl. She could imagine this comment coming from one of the cheerleaders. She rolled her eyes. "I'm black. It comes with the package."

"Beer?"

"Sure." Leah grabbed the light beer he held out to her. Only two hundred calories. She could burn that off in twenty minutes on the treadmill that night.

"Your mama is really something else," Alfreddo said, touching his bottle to hers. "I can't believe she's thirty-six. She looks ten years younger."

Again, Leah had to stifle a laugh with a hefty gulp of the bitter dark beer. Thirty-six! Was that what her mother was telling people now? Please. Victoria had celebrated her forty-fifth birthday that May. Of course no one else knew that information. Apparently in the modeling world, post-thirty was retirement age, but post-forty? You might as well be dead.

"When did your father leave?" Alfreddo drained his beer and buried the bottle in the sand, shaded eyes turning to Leah. The slight curve of his lips dipped lower.

Leah stiffened, all sense of humor gone. "Before I was born," she said. That was a topic her mother refused to ever talk about. And Leah understood why. Her father had apparently left one day in the middle of the night. No note, no explanation. Nothing. Leaving behind his pregnant girlfriend.

"Why?"

Leah's cheeks started to burn, but before she could give Alfreddo a piece of her mind, Cillian saved her.

"That's all for today, everyone! Roald says to wrap this deal up," he called to the crew. "Leah, me love. Could you come here a sec? I need an opinion."

Leah glared at Alfreddo before burying her half-empty beer in the sand and standing up. "Cillian wants me."

"I see that." Alfreddo didn't take his eyes off her as she ran over to the photographer.

"Thanks," she muttered under her breath as she peeked into the viewfinder. It was a picture of a seagull dipping into the ocean. The ordinary act seemed liked art when captured in a photograph.

She'd been flipping through his negatives the whole afternoon. Every shot was creative, with the movement captured perfectly.

"Roald's great but that Alfreddo's a goddamn prick. He's the only reason I feel like quittin' this job and hightailin' it back to Ireland."

Leah laughed. "I wish I had that option. My mom loves him."

"Well, she's insane to let her daughter near a guy like that." Cillian rubbed her bare back, letting his fingers linger. "I'm here with you, you know that, right?"

Her breath shortened when his hands didn't budge after the comforting touch. Up until now, she had assumed this was just innocent flirting, what he did with all the models.

His sea-green eyes said differently. "Pose for me one last time. Lose the sarong."

Leah hesitated. Her stomach was flattish and she wasn't too self-conscious showing it off. Her thighs were a different story. And this guy seemed to like her. She didn't want to turn him off with the sight of her trunklike legs.

"No one else is around, look. I think you're stunning. I promise."

Stunning?

In sixteen years, no one had referred to her as stunning. The guy Leah wanted most in the world had never looked at her with the kind of hungry expression this absolute stranger had.

Why the hell not? Wasn't this why she had wanted to lose weight? Attention like what the other girls got? And everyone else had hightailed it back to the hotel for cocktail hour. Alfreddo had bolted like lightning the second Victoria had shaken the sand off her body.

She unknotted the sarong and winced as it hit the sand.

"Come closer," he said.

Leah obliged with one teeny step forward.

"Closer." He lowered his eyes to the viewfinder. "Perfect. Hold it."

Leah held her breath as he snapped a series of shots.

"These are amazing. You are truly the only woman here today who deserves to be in the catalog. Look at those curves. That's how a real lady is supposed to look."

Leah blushed as she looked at the preview. She looked...okay. Not bad. As she'd thought before, Cillian could make anything look good. Even her.

Cillian was still shaking his head. "Amazing. I am absolutely going to insist to Roald that we use some o' these."

Leah snorted. "Yeah, with Paula and my mother's rolling in the sand pictures, I don't think these stand much of a chance."

"We'll see, won't we?" he said as he started to pack his camera bag.

She started to wrap the sarong around her again.

"Leave it." He grabbed her hand.

Leah started to pull away, but he had a pretty good grip as he wrangled the sarong out of her hand and tossed it behind them.

"Hey! How am I supposed to—"

His lips were on hers before she knew it. She held her breath during the entire kiss and was left, literally, breathless.

"I'm sorry," he murmured after a second. "I couldn't help it."

Leah's pulse was thudding. This, she hadn't expected. She'd always thought that the first guy she hooked up with after she became thin would be Jay. Cillian was an unexpected surprise. She'd been sending him clear signals all day, but didn't expect that a hot, older guy would be interested in her. Make that a hot, older photographer who saw nearly naked models all day and night. And he really did seem to be into her.

"That wasn't the most professional thing, I suppose, right?" Cillian made no effort to move away from her, despite all the nonprofessionalism. Instead he wound his fingers through the ends of her hair.

"You seemed like a professional to me," Leah managed to say.

Cillian's hand traced down her spine, sending chills all the way to her hairline. He lingered on her lower back as his green eyes tangled with her hazel ones. "I don't do this all the time. With all the models. If that's what you were wondering."

Leah shrugged. "You don't owe me an explanation," she said as nonchalantly as possible, although she was secretly thrilled. Maybe he was lying. Maybe he wasn't. The point was that he felt the need to reassure her.

"I feel like I do."

Leah suddenly saw vulnerability in those eyes. She liked it. She liked being able to make a guy feel like that.

"Then." Leah ran a finger down his hairless chest and stopped at the waistband of his board shorts. "Let's argue about it later."

His camera bag slipped to the sand as his other hand cupped the back of her neck and roughly pulled her closer. "I'm pretty sure this is illegal."

"I like illegal." This time she kissed him first, pressing her pelvis against his. It had been almost two years since she'd been with a guy. Her freshman year homecoming date had kissed her good-night at the door…and she'd invited him in for the night. Victoria had been out of town and they had the house to themselves. He'd been slobbery and gropy.

Cillian was not.

His lips nibbled gently on hers, then kissed her

with more intensity, then went back to a gentle nibble. His hands stayed busy, cupping and touching her in ways her body had been craving.

Six weeks ago, she was the constant "best friend." Now this gorgeous man who would never have looked at Fat Leah in the first place couldn't keep his hands off her.

"Is everyone gone?" he whispered as his kisses led them into the sand dune.

"Long gone," Leah whispered, enjoying the silence. No more cheesy hip-hop music, no more photography director screaming instructions. Just the two of them on the partly cloudy day, seagulls crying overhead. The distant roar of a waterfall. Like no one else existed. This felt like a dream.

"Do you have somewhere to be?" With a slight shove, Leah flipped him on his back. Her powerful forearms and shoulders pinned him to the ground as she straddled his thighs.

Those startlingly bright eyes widened in surprise. "You sure about this?"

"You afraid of me?"

"It's not every day a beautiful woman tackles me into the sand and insists on having her way with me."

So this was how it felt to be a "beautiful woman." All of her friends, her mother, everyone else knew how it felt, and today she did, too.

This was worth every minute on the treadmill and every skipped meal.

A surge of power compelled Leah to reach behind her and untie her bikini top.

"Wow." Cillian watched as she raised her arms and threw the top into the sand dune behind them. "You're even more spectacular than I've been fantasizing about."

Leah laughed. A guy was fantasizing about her. Her, Leah Mandeville, best friends to all the guys, but never fantasy material, was being fantasized about.

Victoria had been right. This trip would do her good.

Cillian pulled her down on top of him and cupped her breasts in his hands before rolling over on top of her. She could feel exactly how much he'd been fantasizing against her thigh.

His lips were pressed firmly against hers as his hand slipped inside her bikini bottom. She moaned as his fingertips found a good spot.

"We don't have to rush this, you know."

"I want to."

He was incredible. She was completely ready for him as he readjusted himself on top of her, his shorts lowered to his knees.

"I don't have anything with me," he whispered.

"I don't care," she muttered. "Just go ahead. Please." She wasn't going to interrupt this moment for common sense. So what if she didn't know this guy? For all she knew, he was a complete slut and slept with every model on the beach and she was the only remaining notch on his belt. He could have diseases. Herpes. AIDS.

But in that moment, all she wanted was to be made love to. To feel beautiful and special. To be rewarded for all her hard work losing a full forty-one pounds.

"Leah!"

"Damn," Leah muttered, hoping she was just hearing things.

Cillian stopped his exploration of her body. "Did someone just call your name, love?"

"Leah, I better not catch you out here!" The voice was definitely getting closer. Her mother's voice.

"Leah!" Followed by Alfreddo's.

Damn.

"If I said no, would it make them go away?" Leah sat up and pulled her bikini bottom all the way up to her belly button. "It's Mom and Alfreddo."

Cillian laughed and pulled his shorts up. "Out to spoil all my fun."

"As usual," Leah muttered again.

"Don't pout. What are you doing tomorrow night? Have dinner with me. We'll get room service." His eyes didn't leave hers as he helped her to her feet. "I'll be prepared then."

Leah rumpled his wavy blond hair with her fingertips as she pressed against him for one last kiss. Delicious. "Anything you want. Now help me find my bikini top."

eight

Cruel Intentions
157 lbs

The lobby of the Hotel Diablo was alive with the gentle sway of the indoor palms and the squeaky wheel of the bellboy's cart. The continental breakfast table was lined with an impressive spread of freshly cut fruit and cereal that stood mostly untouched in the early-morning sunlight. The lone sand-and-sun-streaked figure in the lobby was scooping oranges into a bowl when the elevator doors opened with a dramatic swoosh.

Leah practically skipped over to Cillian, happy there was no one else in sight in the waxed marble lobby. Her mother had insisted that she and Leah dine with the models the night before, and she hadn't gotten to see him since their encounter in the sand.

"Good morning," Leah practically purred, posing a little against the table in front of Cillian. Despite the ache in her lower legs from her early-morning run, she was feeling especially confident in a slimming pin-striped tankini with her hair styled in beachy waves. Getting ready had taken almost an hour, but she had been pleased with her reflection when she left the hotel room she was sharing with Victoria.

"Hi." Cillian continued to pour a spoonful of sugar over a bowl of peeled oranges without looking up.

"Sleep well?" Leah glanced around the table. She would eat some blueberries. And a glass of water. A big glass. She had been ridiculously thirsty all night. That would hold her over till lunch, when she would have to put on a show of eating in front of her mother. Leah didn't appreciate her mother picking at a piece of chicken while insisting Leah finish her steak last night at dinner.

Her stomach growled for the first time in days. Not good. She was almost out of Shazan's diet pills and was down to taking only one a day till she got back to L.A. and could get some more.

"How are you?" Cillian turned to pour himself some cranberry juice.

"Sorry I didn't call last night. Mama made me have

dinner with the models." She rolled her eyes. "By having dinner, I mean we sat down at the table, ordered salad and left." It was true. The salads were picked at and the bread basket remained untouched, but all the models insisted they couldn't "eat another bite." Leah had taken a tip from them and followed suit, sipping lemon water and shoving the cut-up pieces of her steak under the plate.

"That sounds about right, then," Cillian said in an unusually subdued voice. "I should get outside to set up."

"We still on for tonight?" Leah glanced around, making sure no one could hear them. No Alfreddo and no Mom. Perfect. She would get to kiss him goodbye.

"Actually—" He turned toward her, eyes a mossy green.

"Actually what?" Leah teasingly said as she grabbed the lapels of his bright red Hawaiian shirt and pulled herself closer. He was so good-looking. Even hotter than Jay. She gently brushed his lips with hers, feeling the tingle all the way down into her toes. No, it hadn't just been her imagination. He really did make her toes curl.

"I have some things to take care of tonight. Work stuff for Roald. Why don't I let you know?" He rested his fingers on hers for a second before pulling her off him.

Leah felt a familiar sinking feeling in her stomach. The same one she got whenever she saw Jay and Jennifer together. Rejection. She knew the feeling well. She let her arms drop. "What's wrong?"

He smiled slightly. "Why do you ask?"

"Because I can tell something's wrong."

"We barely know each other," he murmured and picked up his bowl of oranges.

Leah's sunburnt cheeks suddenly felt very hot. "That's not what you said yesterday."

"Yeah, about that. That was really wrong of me. I'm sorry. I shouldn't have taken advantage of you."

"What the hell are you saying? Nothing happened!" Leah could hear her voice rising. "We were supposed to get together tonight. And you didn't take advantage of me. You know you didn't!"

"I kissed you. I shouldn't have. I really think we should just—"

"What? Pretend nothing happened? Sorry, I won't do that."

Cillian looked around furtively. "We don't want the others to hear—"

"I don't give a damn what others hear. I want to know what changed between yesterday and today."

"Leah, I had a chance to think it over and I realize that—"

"You had me on the ground with my top off!" Leah screeched.

Cillian winced.

Out of her corner of her eye, she could see the concierge walking their way.

"That was wrong of me. You're only sixteen." Cillian wiped his hands on the sides of his shorts and whispered, "I'm sorry, Leah, but this is a really bad idea. You're a kid!"

"Yeah, I get it. I was a kid yesterday, too, by the way. What is it, really? Is it because I'm not thin? If that's the case, I want to hear you—" Leah punched him in the arm, hard "—say it!"

"No! No, no! You're amazing. Really, you are."

"Yeah, I bet. That's why you can't get away from me fast enough. Look at you. Backing away." It was true. He'd taken ten steps back during their conversation, having long abandoned his bowl of oranges.

"Well, you're beating me up. What do you expect me to—"

"You're a moron." Leah had tears in her eyes that she wasn't about to show him as she stomped away, leaving the blueberries behind. She'd been right. He wasn't interested in her. No doubt there was some sort of bet among the photographers over who would pick up the "fat girl."

She couldn't keep the tears back as she ran up to the room.

I hate my body. Everyone hates this body.

Why couldn't she be thin like the other girls? Guys like Cillian would die to be with her. They wouldn't dump her after seeing her body.

If you only lost ten pounds, he would notice you. Victoria's words were so true. Except it wasn't just ten pounds. It wasn't even forty pounds. She had to keep losing. She wasn't thin enough yet.

She slammed the door of the hotel room, startling Victoria into dropping her eyeliner brush. "What happened?"

For an instant, Leah wanted to throw herself into her mother's arms and tell her the whole story. Jay, the cheerleaders, Cillian. How she was having trouble losing even a pound that week.

But Victoria would tell her to put all those thoughts aside and focus on the photo shoot they would be in in a few weeks. After all, what was school and a social life compared to Demi and Tallulah?

"They have a ton of donuts downstairs. Nothing healthy at all," Leah fibbed before throwing herself on the bed. "I'll just get, like, a parfait or something from room service and then come down to the beach, okay?"

"Fine. Don't be long." Victoria slipped her feet into gold sandals and knotted a silky pink sarong around her narrow hips. "Seems to me you had a good time yesterday. Fit right in."

"Uh-huh," Leah muttered, burying her head into a pillow. Yeah, right. Fit right in. Like a homecoming queen at a car wash.

"I'll ask Cillian to take some photos for your portfolio. He is an extremely talented photographer, even though he's just an assistant right now."

Leah was silent until her mother left the room. She didn't want to face Cillian; she didn't want to face the world.

I hate myself. I hate myself.

She tore at her hair. Why was this happening to her? Why wasn't anything she did enough?

I hate myself.

She just wanted to hide in bed until the whole horrible weekend was over. Back home, what awaited her? She had to go home and see Jay again. With Jennifer on his arm.

I hate my life. I wish I was dead.

She pressed her balled fists against her eye sockets. What had gone wrong? How had she gotten to this point where she was sobbing her eyes out in a hotel room over a guy she barely knew not wanting to be with her because she was *fat?*

Why did she even care? She was better than this, she didn't need to care.

But the rest of the world does care. You want to be alone for the rest of your life because you're too lazy to make an effort?

No.

She would continue to lose weight. She would lose weight until every single person that mattered noticed.

The telltale *bing* of her laptop signaled a new e-mail message. Leah reached for the computer and sat up in bed, smudging away tears in the process. She'd been e-mailing regularly with the girl who had suggested the watermelon diet on the ANArexia Web site. All the other girls seemed a little crazy and obsessive, but this girl, DietDiva, seemed to be in Leah's boat. She wanted to lose a few pounds before prom and was trying every technique out there without being stupid.

Hey, BBGirl! How did the watermelon diet work out for you? I lost like 15 pounds in the past two weeks. I fit a size 2 now! What about you?—DietDiva

Size 2? Yeah, right, not even close. Leah frowned.

Hey, DietDiva. I'm down to about a tight size 4 after a week of watermelon. I can't handle it anymore, though. I need to get down to a 0 in the next month. My modeling thing is in three weeks! Any other ideas?—BBGirl

PS: Men SUCK!

Leah waited for a few minutes, but got no answer. She sighed. She was just so tired and achy. She'd woken up early to run on the treadmill in the hotel gym for an hour, and her shins had been screaming at her all morning. Plus, she was so thirsty again. She would close her eyes for just a few minutes and then go down to the beach.

"Leah!" The voice sounded very far away.

"Go 'way…" Leah mouthed the words, but didn't hear them come out of her mouth.

"Leah!" The voice was coming closer.

Leah pried open an eye. It wasn't a dream; her mother was calling her. "What is it?"

"What's going on here?" Victoria was standing over her, illuminated in light from the bedside lamp. The room seemed dark otherwise. She didn't remember closing the blinds.

"Just taking a nap. I said I'd come down."

There was silence and then the bed tilted as Victoria sat down next to Leah. "That was ten hours ago."

"What!" Leah's head spun as she sat up. "I slept the whole day?"

The spinning continued and Leah laid her head back down. She felt as though she was going to faint.

Victoria ran a hand over the pillow Leah was lying on. "Are you sure you're feeling okay? Is there something you'd like to tell me?"

"I was just…so tired. I don't know—" Leah yawned "—what's wrong with me. Sorry, Mama."

Victoria held up a fistful of hair. "You're losing hair. A lot of it. How did this happen?"

Leah lifted her body off the bed and noticed the wads of hair that had gathered on her pillow. "Oh my God."

She recalled tearing at her hair in a fit of rage earlier that afternoon. How had it come off her head so easily? She ran her fingers through her hair and several strands clung to her fingers.

"What is this, your hair—"

"Oh my God!" Leah sprang to the floor and winced as her shins nearly gave out. The room spun again and Leah grabbed on to the bedside table. What was happening to her?

"—is literally falling out of your head, Leah!"

"Mama!" Leah clutched at the strands of hair that continued to fall from her scalp every time she touched it.

"I think we better get you downstairs for a good, solid dinner. I don't want to hear any of that 'just a salad for me' nonsense today. When your hair starts to fall out like this, it's a real problem. A vitamin deficiency."

Leah was still staring in horror at the clumps of

wavy black hair on the bed. She felt around on her head for any bald spots. Thank God, nothing yet. How had this happened? It had to be the hotel shampoo. Cheap-asses!

Ten minutes later, both Mandevilles were clad in black dresses and were in the elevator on the way to the lobby restaurant. Leah gazed at the deep purplish hollows under her eyes that concealer hadn't been able to cover up. At least her cheekbones were defined, something she had never been able to accomplish before.

"There she is." Alfreddo's voice reached Leah before she could focus on the table where the crew was sitting. Alfreddo, Victoria's model friends, Paula and Juliette, Abby the director, a few of the lighting guys…and Cillian. Great. The knot of worry in Leah's stomach seemed to tighten. She didn't want to face him, not in front of all these people.

Victoria took the seat next to Alfreddo, leaving Leah to sit across from Cillian.

"You feeling okay?" Cillian murmured.

Leah ignored him and picked up the menu. She felt nauseated just thinking of this food. Leg of lamb in Moroccan spices, chicken with lime and cilantro, fried shrimp and chips basket.

Disgusting.

Leah dropped the menu. All she wanted was water.

"The lamb is excellent," Cillian commented.

Leah ignored him and turned to her mother and Alfreddo. "How was the shoot? Any fiascos?"

"Absolutely none." Alfreddo grinned and put an arm around Victoria. "We did miss you, though. Are you feeling all right? Did something happen?"

Leah could feel the probing eyes of everyone on her. Did they all know about Cillian? How she had thrown herself at him and how he had rejected her? Had he told them?

"Are you feeling all right?"

Leah shot a withering glance in Cillian's direction as he asked the question. Jackass. Yeah, a girl recovered from being dumped in approximately twelve hours. That's how things worked. "The heat. I, uh, got sunstroke."

Victoria frowned, but before she could comment, the waiter arrived, notebook in hand.

Everyone placed their orders quickly. When it came time for Leah, she was ready with her standard answer of a side salad and a tall glass of lemon water.

Victoria cut her off. "My daughter and I will both have the leg of lamb. I'll have a glass of wine and she will have a vanilla cream soda."

Leah opened her mouth to protest. That would be two thousand calories. At least!

"Mom," she whispered.

"We'll talk about this later," Victoria said quietly.

An uneasy silence fell over the table.

Leah could feel her cheeks heating up again. Why was Victoria doing this to her? She'd been on Leah's case to lose weight for years. And now she was so close to fitting a perfect size 4 and her mother was sabotaging her. Was she actually threatened by her daughter? Well, it wasn't going to work. Leah wasn't going to touch a single bite.

She drank a whole glass of water as the conversation started back up. Cillian blathered about his light and how great his boss was, the models went on and on about how "fat" and "pasty" the other models were, Alfreddo made everything sound sleazy.

Business as usual.

The lamb arrived and Leah scowled at it.

"It's really very good," Cillian added helpfully.

"Really? I thought it was bad. That's why they're charging more than your annual paycheck for it," Leah snarked at him.

He frowned and dug a fork into his peppercorn-sauce-covered steak.

After a few moments, the scent of the cardamom got to Leah and she picked up her fork. It was protein. She could have a small bite. This would help her shins heal faster so she could get back to running.

The lamb seemed to melt in her mouth and Leah

almost moaned with pleasure. She hadn't tasted that kind of flavor in weeks. It was divine. She took another bite and set down her fork as she chewed.

So good.

She took another bite and realized what she was doing. She'd played into her mother's hands. She had to stop eating without making it look too obvious.

Victoria was gesturing toward Paula with her fork and talking to Alfreddo about *Jade* magazine's November spread. Everyone else's eyes were on Victoria. As usual.

Leah raised her napkin to her lips and spit the remains of the lamb into it. Just as she was about to lower the napkin, Cillian's eyes caught hers and Leah froze. Did he know what she was up to?

Who cared? If he even thought about telling, she had far better blackmail material info on him.

She took a few more bites of lamb during the rest of the meal in between spits and left her Italian soda untouched. She rested her fingers on her lower belly. Still flat. She was okay. She was doing just fine.

"Cillian, darling." Victoria's friend Paula leaned back in her chair and touched Cillian's shoulder. "You know that yoga move you were showing me in my room last night? Which body part is that for?"

"Lower back." Cillian rose from his chair and rested his hands on Paula's back. "These muscles get extremely tight and the cobra just loosens them up. Like this."

Leah averted her eyes to the dessert menu in front of her. This explained things. Last night Cillian hadn't been waiting by the phone for her call. He had been practicing "yoga moves" with Paula in her hotel room.

Leah bit her lip as tears threatened to fill her eyes. She was not going to cry in front of these people. She was better than this. She could feel herself losing control. She didn't know what was up with her emotions lately. It felt as if she were on a hormonal roller coaster.

"Dessert, anyone?" The waiter arrived to clear the table.

"I'll have a crème brûlée," Leah said before she could stop herself.

All heads at the table swiveled in her direction.

"To be young again," Paula sighed. "I haven't tasted a dessert in eighteen years."

Of course she hadn't. Leah felt blood rushing to her head. And that was why Paula had the cute photographer in her hotel room at night instead of Leah.

The crème brûlée arrived in record time and the whipped cream seemed to stare Leah in the face. All eyes on the table still on her, she took a bite.

"It's fantastic. Does anyone want any?" She forced a smile.

All heads shook.

One more bite. Just to show them up. Leah scraped the side of the dish and poised the spoon in front of her mouth. She could swear everyone was holding their breaths to see if she would really consume all those calories willingly.

She popped the spoon into her mouth.

And took another bite. A big one.

The perfectly whipped custard was too much for Leah to take. Within minutes, the dish was empty.

She sat back, stunned, staring at the empty dish until Victoria tapped her on the shoulder to go upstairs.

What had she done?

Leah groaned as she unlocked the door of the hotel room. Sacrificing a month of hard work for a crème brûlée.

"I'm going out for a bit." Victoria hurried in behind her and exchanged her stilettos for flat sandals. "Alfreddo and I'll only be a little while. He wants to take a walk on the beach. To talk about work."

Leah felt ill at the thought of Victoria and Alfreddo. Hand in hand on the beach.

"Sure, Mom, go ahead," Leah muttered and flopped backward onto the twin bed. She had other things to worry about.

Victoria was gone in a puff of perfume.

Why had she done it? For just two minutes of incredible happiness, she was going to gain back a week's worth of hard work.

She was so stupid.

"I'm a moron," she muttered and forced herself to sit up. Maybe there was a way to undo it. Some workout she could do tomorrow or some food she could not eat that would undo it.

She logged in to her e-mail account to see if DietDiva had responded. No answer yet. She surfed to the ANArexia Web site to see if DietDiva was online.

She skimmed over all the old posts and was disappointed to see there were no new diets to try.

Two members online for chat.

Why not?

I feel so full tonight. I got dessert. I can't believe I did that! I've been so good.

She hit Send and waited. Nothing.

Oh, well, she was just about to go to ESPN.com when a blinking window caught her eye.

Hey, BBGirl! I know what you mean! That same thing happened to me last night! I was at graduation and I couldn't help but have a piece of cake! God, I feel so bad!

The girl's name was Wannabe.

Excitable. Jeez.

What'd you do? Leah typed back.

When I feel that full, I just make myself throw up. No more worries!

Leah blinked. Throwing up? Disgusting, yet... obvious. It was *so* obvious. If she overate, she could get rid of it. Just like that. So easy.

Thanks, she typed slowly. She logged off.

Throwing up on a regular basis was a problem. They'd learned all about it in health class. A disease. You could die from doing that.

But she wasn't doing that here. It was just a onetime thing. It was like being sick. She's eaten something bad and had to get it out of her body.

She flipped on the light switch in the bathroom. Already she could see her cheeks were puffing back up. No wonder Cillian had dumped her. He'd realized there was no way he could be seen with a fat girl like her in his field. She let these calories sit in her body and she would be a hundred and seventy pounds by morning. No. Not a chance.

She stuck her finger down her throat and leaned over the toilet.

nine

Fight Club
151 lbs

Leah should've felt sick on the drive from O.C. back to L.A. The stop-and-go traffic and the way Alfreddo kept caressing Victoria's leg as he drove should have made her ill and dizzy.

But it didn't.

She'd never felt so fantastic in her life. A hundred and fifty-one pounds. Despite the dessert eating, she had lost around five pounds over the course of the weekend.

Her mood darkened for a second, thinking of Cillian, but she tossed those thoughts out the car window along with a sugar-free gum wrapper.

"Why don't we have dinner together tonight,

girls?" Alfreddo turned around just in time to watch the gum wrapper bounce down the freeway. Instead of a lecture about a litter-free earth, he smiled that Cheshire cat grin of his. "Me and the two loveliest ladies in L.A. at the Ivy."

Food again! Could no one think of anything else? No way was she eating in front of people again. She was *not* going to have another dessert shoved down her throat.

"Yeah, I have homework," Leah said at the same time as Victoria accepted the invitation saying, "Alfreddo, you're a doll. We would love to."

"Mama, really. I've been gone all weekend. I have a geometry test tomorrow and I'm not prepared at all. I need to read this book for English that's really boring, and—what, you want me to fail school and have to repeat the eleventh grade?"

"Just you and I tonight, darling, then," Alfreddo purred and put his hand back on Victoria's leg.

Victoria gave Leah a *look* in the rearview mirror. "When I get home, I want to see *all* the homework you've finished."

Leah rolled her eyes. "Whatever," she muttered.

Twenty minutes later, the Benz pulled up outside the Mandevilles' house. Leah noted the day was still sunny and light. Perfect. A long run, and then she'd get to work on her studying.

"Have fun! Don't end up in the *Enquirer* for making out in the bathroom!" Leah grabbed her duffel bag and slammed the car door before Victoria could change her mind.

Her mother was dating Alfreddo. Openly and obviously at that. Their cuddles and stupid lovey-dovey talk had crossed the line of agent-model long ago, but today's open grope-fest and dinner date made it official.

Leah cringed. Her mother had almost married the last guy she'd dated. A creep with a goatee and a gold tooth who leered at her. And anything else female and moving. Alfreddo wasn't much of a step up.

She ran into the house and dropped her luggage in the kitchen. She scooped up Espresso Bean and gave the cat a kiss on the nose.

"Hi, baby. Miss me? I missed you tons. L.A. is full of jackasses."

Meow. The cat seemed to agree.

"Yeah, you're right. Screw them."

Grabbing the Ziploc bag of diet pills out of her bag, Leah counted them. She'd taken one every day during the weekend. She only had three left. She popped one with a big glass of water and laced up her running shoes, wincing at the sharp pain in her shins. She thought she would have recovered by now. Usually her aches and pains were gone by the end of the day.

She bent and flexed her right foot, trying to stretch the shin.

"Ouch."

Maybe it wasn't a good idea to put any more pressure on her shins. Maybe her homework *should* come first today. She had to finish *How to Ruin a Summer Vacation* by tomorrow for a quiz and she was still on the acknowledgments page.

But the modeling shoot. Just three weeks away. She still had to get into a size 0. Damn sample sizes. And maybe there was a chance of returning the size-large Snow Ball dress and getting a smaller size and redeeming herself in Shazan's eyes. It was certainly no coincidence that she hadn't heard much from her friend after the dress-shopping fiasco.

No, she had to get in a workout. Pain or no pain.

She plugged her Zune MP3 player into her ears. She had her Beyoncé and her Shakira. She was ready for her miles.

A wolf whistle greeted Leah as she emerged from the house in her brand-new workout clothes. A black midriff-baring tank top and low-riding striped shorts. It was the most revealing outfit she had ever owned, but it looked pretty okay on her. Good even, apparently, given Jay's whistle.

"What do you want?" Leah asked, keeping her voice as cold as her muscles. "I need to get going."

She was in no mood to bicker with him about movie lines. He could act as though everything was normal, but she wasn't good enough of a liar to do it, too.

Jay didn't move, continuing to stare at her while the hose he was using to wash his Mustang leaked water onto the driveway.

Staring at her the way a man stared at a woman. Not the way a friend stared at a friend. Finally.

"Your hose is leaking." Leah smirked, not able to resist the obvious double entendre.

"You look great. Have you been on your diet? These are really cool, by the way." Jay reached over and removed her headphones from her ears. "Where did you go all weekend? I looked for you yesterday."

"The L.A. modeling thing." She grabbed the headphones back from him. "These came with the Zune."

"Well, you look great. All tan. You're kind of like a cross between Beyoncé and Shakira in that new song."

Leah couldn't help but blush. He knew they were her favorites. "You're so full of it."

Jay grinned. "I mean it. I hardly recognized you." He shoved his hands into the pockets of his camouflage cargo shorts. "Listen—"

"Jay! Come for dinner *beta!*" The telltale screech of Mrs. Dalal initiated in the kitchen and reached the driveway with hardly any decibel loss.

"Ma, come on!" Jay whined in return. Loudly.

"Jay! No more nonsense, come in at once." Mrs. Dalal, a tiny, yet impressive woman with a dish towel tucked into the front of her sari appeared in the doorway. "Is that Leah talking to you? My God, she's so thin. Ask her to come in as well, please. We need to put some food in her."

"Ma."

"Mrs. Dalal, really, I have to finish my run. And I have so much homework!"

"Leah, you must come in for dinner. I've made chicken *biryani!*" With that she disappeared.

"Coming, Ma," Jay called back and turned to Leah. "And you better, too, if you know what's good for you."

"My run!"

"Later. You do not want to annoy a small Asian woman. It will not end well."

The ends of Leah's lips twitched. She had missed Jay. And his family. And the countless dinners she'd had at their place. The Dalal clan was a homey group of people, and being in their house instantly made you a member of their family...parental scolding included. "All right. But I won't eat anything."

Leah thought she heard Jay snort as he opened the front door for her.

* * *

"God, your poor cousin. You think they'll really marry him off to some random girl?" Leah leaned against the pillar on the front porch, still wiping tears from her eyes. She hadn't remembered laughing like that in ages. Jay's cousin had been visiting, and all the family had talked about was his pending arranged marriage. The poor sap sat quietly in the corner the whole night while everyone argued over whether his future wife should be able to cook *and* sing, or was just cooking acceptable?

Luckily everyone had been so busy torturing the poor kid that no one noticed that Leah had pushed her food around for half an hour and had cleared her plate in the kitchen before anyone else had gotten up.

"He's kind of a schmuck, so he might go for it. An arranged marriage, I mean."

Leah watched Jay swat at a fly circling the lone bulb on the porch. Despite his all-American-boy attitude, she knew he valued his cultures and traditions. "What about you? You think you'll get arranged off? Not now. I mean when you're old."

"God, I hope not." Jay laughed. "I hope I won't be such a loser that I'll need my parents to find me a wife."

"Well, you will be a loser, but don't worry, girls like that. You'll have plenty of options."

Crickets serenaded them as a gentle breeze blew

strands of Leah's wavy hair across her face. Jay caught hold of the ends of a lock. "I like your hair like this."

Leah reached out and removed the strand from his fingertips, her hand touching his. "All for you." Her tone was sarcastic, but her words weren't.

She wanted to ask about Jennifer. Were they still together? If so, was he just playing with Leah out here tonight?

She was too afraid of the answers.

"I really need to go," she sighed. She hadn't done her homework. She hadn't run her five miles. But the night had been worth it.

Jay kissed her forehead. "Good night, babe. Ride with me tomorrow?"

Ignoring the thudding of the heart, she placed a hand on her hip and was surprised to feel the jut of a hip bone.

"We'll see. I have a line of hot guys from O.C. coming to see me." Leah tucked the loose strands of hair behind her ear. "They're all into tall bikini models."

"I wouldn't be surprised in the least." Jay's eyes traveled over her again.

Leah brushed a hand up against his cheek and let it rest there for an instant. As she moved closer, the bare skin of her stomach grazed his belt. She touched her full lips to the stubble on his cheek. "Night."

She could feel his eyes watching her as she walked away. He was still standing still as she reached her kitchen door. There was no way he could say they were "just friends" after that encounter.

Leah was still smiling as she unlocked her kitchen door. Her plan was working. By the time the photo shoot came around, Jennifer would be long gone. If she wasn't already.

"Bye-bye, China Doll," Leah murmured, twirling on her toes as she entered the kitchen.

She nearly screamed when she saw a hunched figure sitting at the counter.

Victoria stood up, arms crossed.

"Damn, you scared the hell out of me!"

Victoria ignored her and gestured toward a Ziploc bag on the counter. "Explain this."

The pills.

"Just some diet pills," Leah huffed. God, she'd almost had a heart attack. What the hell was Victoria doing? Her heart was still racing.

"Why are you taking them? Do you know how dangerous they are? These aren't over-the-counter. Where did you get them?"

"A friend." Leah attempted to grab the bag back. "What's your problem? You take stuff like this all the time."

"I take vitamins."

"All right, Mama. Whatever you say. Weight-loss vitamins." Leah rolled her eyes.

"Excuse me?" One hand was on Victoria's hip. Now Leah knew where she got that from.

"You heard me! You're always on some crazy diet or another, but when I do it, you can't stand it!" Leah was losing her patience with this whole thing. She could feel herself starting to boil over. "You don't want me to lose weight. You want me to be a loser at the modeling thing."

"Leah, what you're doing is dangerous. Don't you understand that? I see what's happening. I've seen it happen to too many models. The not-eating, these violent mood swings. The hair loss. Do you see that fine hair growing on your arms? Do you know what that is?"

Leah froze as she saw the arm hair. That was new.

"It's called lanugo hair. It happens when your body starts to shut down from lack of food. I understand these signs. Believe me, I do."

Leah glanced at her arm and back at Victoria. Her mother was thin, perfect. All without trying. How did she understand?

"Don't make stuff up, okay? You want me to be fat at the shoot? You're the one that wanted me to be in it so bad! I need to be a size 0. You heard those *Jade* people!"

"There is a line—" Victoria attempted to lay a hand on Leah's arm.

Leah shook it off and clenched her fists. "No. There isn't. Either I'm thin or I'm not. Decide, Mama. Now. Decide and let it go. If it wasn't for me, you would never get this golden opportunity. You're a has-been without me and you know it. You can go around and tell everybody you're thirty-five, but do you really think anyone believes it?"

Victoria closed her eyes and Leah thought she saw her lips tremble.

"I do not need to hear your mouth. There are safe ways to lose the weight. These pills?" Victoria held up the bag. "Do you know what they are? They're from Mexico and eat up your stomach lining. They cause heart attacks, strokes. Completely illegal in the U.S."

Leah fumed. Resorting to lies. Shazan had been taking them for months. She was smart. She was the valedictorian of the class. She would never take something illegal.

"Which of your friends got them for you? I need to speak to their parents right now."

"You're such a nut job!" Leah burst out.

"Little girl—"

"You're freaking schizo! No wonder Dad left! You're so obsessed with being thin! All you care about is your career! And when I try to do the same—"

"Is that what you think? Your father left because I was focused on my career?"

"Obviously, *Mother!*" Leah sneered, all traces of remorse gone. This had been coming for weeks and there was no going back now. "You lie about your age. You sleep with these creeps to get ahead—"

Slap!

Leah grabbed her cheek. Her mother had never touched her. Not once. How dare she slap her now? When Leah was doing everything possible to make their lives better?

"Your father left because I was anorexic. Right after you were born, I was desperate to get back into my old body. He left because I refused to admit I had a problem and *your* health was suffering. He refused to watch me self-destruct. So he left."

Leah sucked in her breath. Anorexic? Her mother? Like the girls on the Web site?

"I see the same signs in you, Leah. This disease is passed on genetically. We have to get you to a doctor. Tomorrow morning."

She wasn't like that. She wasn't skinny and crazy and...obsessive. She was normal. She was finally starting to fit in.

"I am not you, Mama." Leah reached for the bag of pills.

"No, you aren't." Victoria crumpled the bag in her hand. "And I won't let you become me."

ten

Kill Bill
148 lbs

"WE need to talk about your performance." Coach Jenna Richards was an athletic woman who had been the star of Sonoma High's basketball team when she had attended the school ten years prior. The coach's boyish figure and a pixie haircut almost made her look as young as the rest of the Sonoma Snow Leopards basketball team, and Leah had always felt at ease with her.

However, today, the slender woman looked almost menacing as she closed her office door behind Leah. As menacing as her mother had looked when she'd scheduled Leah for a doctor's appointment that afternoon. A full physical. It made Leah ill to even think about it. The doctor would poke and prod at her like a piece of meat.

There was nothing wrong with her. Why didn't people understand that?

Leah had braced herself for the worst ever since she'd received the coach's e-mail that morning. Today was the game that would define whether Sonoma High School was going to be in the all-state finals. Leah needed to concentrate. She didn't have time for yet another lecture from judgmental adults who thought they knew everything.

"What about my performance?" Leah crossed one ankle over the opposite knee and winced. Her ankles and shins were still sore. Elevation and an ice pack hadn't helped one bit. The pain, combined with two diet pills, had made her completely lose her appetite for the day and she'd only had a small cup of soup for lunch.

"You've been very distracted on the court lately. Missing passes, playing less offense." Coach sat down behind her desk and ran her fingers through her longish bangs. "Plus, you've lost quite a bit of weight and I fear it's affecting those amazing jump shots you're capable of. Your strength has dramatically depleted. I know you can tell."

"Coach, I'm faster and stronger than any of the—"

"I know you are. I am not disputing you are the star of this team, but, Leah, you need to be the star on the court. Our team *and* our opposition. From what I understand, you still want to play ball in college, correct?"

Leah nodded sullenly.

The coach tapped her short, squared-off fingernails on the desk, French manicure glistening. "The scouts will come around next year for sure if we win the state champs this year. Don't you want that guarantee? We won't win the champs unless you're in top form."

The statement should have made Leah feel good. Instead, it added another layer to the burden she was already carrying. Modeling shoot, schoolwork, being thin, Victoria and now the game.

"A few weeks ago, I had no doubt in my mind that we could beat East L.A. in the finals. They are good, but you are very good. Now I'm not sure."

She sat back and crossed her hands on her flat abdomen. "Is there something you'd like to talk about? Purely confidential, of course. We'll leave your mother and the team out of it."

Looking into Coach's sparkly aqua eyes, Leah was reminded that she wasn't that old. She must have gone through all this stuff just a few years ago. She would understand.

Or not.

She would most likely throw Leah off the team if

she found out about the pills, the extreme dieting… and definitely, the purging.

"I'll do better, Coach." Leah sighed. "Promise."

"Sorry, that's not good enough. I want you to see a doctor."

Leah glanced down at her feet, squeezed into a pair of Victoria's Christian Louboutin heels. They went perfectly with the skinny jeans and fitted blazer she was wearing. Finally, she was able to wear clothes that girls in magazines wore and have them not look stupid on her.

And everyone wanted to ruin it.

"Mom's got me scheduled for an appointment this afternoon."

Coach frowned.

"I'm serious. You can call her and ask if you want. I'll get a note for you tomorrow."

Coach didn't look convinced but gave a little nod. "I'll let you play today. Plus, Leah, if I don't get a note by Monday, you're benched. I've seen too many girls like you fall into the anor—"

"I'm fine." Leah stood up abruptly. She didn't want to hear that word again.

Anorexic. AN. OR. EX. IC.

Such an ugly word.

"Leah."

Leah paused before opening the office door.

"Please come to me if you have something to say, okay? Just between us."

"Sure, Coach."

Leah jogged to the girls' locker room to suit up, groaning in pain with every step. The coach was right about one thing. She hadn't made a jump shot in a while. She hadn't won a game for the team in a while. Today would be different. No matter what, they were going to win.

Plus, Jay had mentioned he would probably come to see her play. He'd been surprisingly subdued after last weekend's encounter on his porch, but Leah blamed it on finals week.

Leah waved to the girls, who were all standing around and gossiping about the other team, who were already warming up on the court. She swallowed nervously. They had to kick some serious ass today. They had to get to the finals. Otherwise, she and the coach would be having another conversation, which was not going to end as easily as today's had.

Plus, she had a doctor's appointment today.

Leah spotted Shazan sitting on a bench alone, looking as if she were swimming in her cheerleading outfit. Good, if anyone could make her feel better, it was Shazan. She needed a good pep talk and she would be ready to roll.

"What's the word?" Leah flopped down on the

bench and stared hard at the ceiling. *Visualization. Imagine yourself winning. Imagine yourself making that winning shot.*

"Hi," Shazan said quietly.

"I'm in so much trouble," Leah muttered to her friend as she laced up her shoes.

Shazan sniffed and Leah realized she was crying.

"What's wrong? Hey, what happened?" Leah gave Shazan a little shake. She had never seen her friend lose her composure before. Shazan was always poised, pretty and perfect. Now her nose was red and she kept dabbing her eyes with a tissue.

Shazan sighed. "He broke up with me."

"Who? What! Why?"

Shazan's attempted smile failed badly. "I don't know. Bill just said this wasn't working and it's over. A month before the Snow Ball and he dumps me. This morning."

"I'm so sorry. I don't know what the hell he's thinking. I mean, you're so incredibly—ugh. He was a lucky bastard and he ruined it."

Tears started to escape Shazan's eyes. "He didn't even give a reason."

Leah wrapped an arm around Shazan's shoulders and hugged her tightly. "Oh, he'll give a reason. While I beat him up, he'll give plenty of reasons."

Shazan laughed and fished around in the purse for some more tissues and her diet pill bottle.

Leah blinked when she saw the pill bottle. It had been completely full three days ago when Shazan had supplied her with enough for the week. Now there was just one pill left. How many had Shazan taken that week? Leah remembered her mother's words. *Illegal in the U.S. Very bad side effects.*

Shazan sipped from her water bottle and swallowed the lone pill. Leah wasn't about to lecture her friend on the hazards of diet pill overuse today.

"I don't know what to do." Shazan blew her nose into a tissue. "Damn. A nosebleed. Great."

Leah stared in alarm as blood continued to leak from her friend's nose. "Are you sure you're okay?"

"Yeah. It's just dry in here."

"Come on." Leah stood and held out her hand. "We need to get you cleaned up before the game. Don't worry about Bill. I'm going to kill him."

The San Diego Tigers were leading by two when the ten-second buzzer rang.

Leah had sworn she wouldn't let it happen, but the Tigers had gotten past her three times already. Not anymore. The first time, she had leaped in the air to block a shot and had lost her balance on a weak ankle on the landing.

The second time she hadn't been quick enough to block Jemima Kane.

The third time she just hadn't been paying attention, instead looking to the stands to see if Jay was there cheering her on.

He wasn't. And Lisa May, the weakest member of the Tigers, had gotten by her. Something that had never happened before.

And would not happen again.

Leah grabbed the ball in midair after Allison passed it to her. Steady dribbles led her to the San Diego girls' basket. Too many people blocking her already. She would have to make this shot from here.

She arced the ball through the air and Jemima, the star defense, leaped into the air and blocked it.

Leah backtracked quickly and covered Jemima as the shorter, more compact girl wove through the court. Leah managed to knock the ball out of her hands and passed to Julia DeLouis.

Julia looked surprised Leah had actually trusted her and quickly dribbled toward the Tigers' basket. She scored the basket easily.

Leah felt proud yet terrified. Julia DeLouis was outscoring her this game. No good.

Ah.

Leah was hit with a dizzy spell and leaned on her quads to keep from falling.

What was wrong with her? The whole room seemed to spin. Everything was fuzzy as if she were in a dream.

Leah shook her head violently. Not now. She needed to win this game. And Jemima was heading straight toward her, ball in hand. Jemima faked left.

Leah fell for it. And watched openmouthed as Jemima made a three-pointer.

This was not going to happen. She was not going to lose this game. No way in hell. This Jemima had to go. She had made ninety percent of the other team's shots. Leah had to take her out of commission.

Leah waited until Jemima paused for another throw and ran full force into the girl. Leah very deliberately pulled her knee back and down, and slammed straight into Jemima's knee.

Shrieking, Jemima hit the floor. Leah fell backward as well, feigning pain.

The ref's whistle blew and Leah spotted only a few raised eyebrows from her team. The chances of anyone knowing she'd done that on purpose were slim. She'd never hurt another player before, but it had to be done.

Plus, she hated Jemima's hard body complete with six-pack abs.

After a few minutes of chaos, Leah was benched and Jemima was carried off the court by her teammates. Leah watched someone fetch Jemima an ice pack as she groaned with pain when she tried to bend her knee.

"God," Coach Richards muttered. "What the hell is happening to my team?"

"Sorry, Coach," Leah muttered as she rested her chin in her hands.

"We'll talk about this later." Coach had her eyes on the court, where Allison and Julia were working on the next play. "It's up to the two of them to win this game now."

Leah sat down heavily on the bleachers and looked over at a commotion in the corner. Shazan was standing nose to nose with Bill Collins in the corner. Both looked furious.

"...have a problem...need help!" Bill was waving his hands.

"...nothing wrong with me!" Shazan yelled back.

Leah frowned. What could they be fighting about? Why couldn't he just leave her alone?

She was about to get up and intervene, but a warning look from the coach stopped her. She watched the rest of the game from lowered eyelashes. With Jemima no longer in the game, Sonoma was easily able to score four points in the remaining five seconds.

Unsurprisingly, Leah was called back into the coach's office instead of the victory ice-cream outing. She was secretly relieved not to have to pretend to enjoy a scoop of fat-free vanilla as a show for the other girls.

"That was insane. I've never seen you do anything like that before." Coach slammed the door behind Leah. "What the hell was that?"

"Coach, I—"

"What? It was an accident? It wasn't deliberate? Go ahead, Leah, please keep lying to me."

"It was an accident. I was just blocking her and I, you know, misjudged my strength. I'm pretty strong. You know that. I got hurt, too, you know."

Coach shook her head. "I'm taking you out of the next game."

Leah shot to her feet. "Coach! Come on! We're in the finals! The next game is crucial!"

"I cannot tolerate this behavior, Leah. Now, I'm sorry, but—"

The phone rang.

Leah flopped back into the chair as the coach held up a finger and motioned for her to stay.

What the hell was this? She was supposed to win at any cost. She had enabled the team to win. Jemima would be fine. What the heck was the big deal?

"I understand. I'll be right there." Coach pressed the Off button.

"Coach, I—"

"They've gone to the hospital."

Leah stopped short. "Who has?"

The coach set the phone into the cradle and looked at Leah, her deep blue eyes troubled and sad. "Shazan Ali and her family. She collapsed in the locker room just now. The paramedics said she's had a heart attack."

eleven

A Mighty Heart
148 lbs

Leah rode with Coach Richards to the East Sonoma Hospital's emergency room without asking for permission. After following the coach into her SUV, Leah climbed into the passenger's side. Not a word was spoken between the two as tires peeled out of the parking lot.

The ride to the hospital was agonizing because of the rush-hour L.A. traffic and the sunken feeling in Leah's stomach. This was her fault. She had known something was wrong this morning when she saw the empty pill bottle. She should have said something to someone. She should have talked to Shazan and insisted she sit the game out. She should have done something.

Shazan was the only one who really understood what Leah was going through. Shazan was the only one who supported her. Leah couldn't lose her now.

Leah realized she was crying when the coach silently handed her a package of Kleenex.

"Coach—"

"You need to stay strong right now and not fall apart in front of her parents." The coach made a severe turn into the hospital's driveway.

Leah was out of the car before it was in Park.

"Shazan Ali's room, please." Leah was panting by the time she located the receptionist's desk. Why hospitals were so difficult to navigate was beyond her. When people were desperate to see their loved ones, a labyrinth wasn't the kind of obstacle they wanted to deal with.

The receptionist popped her gum and blinked at Leah, her puzzled look indicating that she did not understand the question.

"Look, Jiffy," Leah said, reading her name tag. "She's my friend. She was brought in for having a…she had a heart attack. I need to know where she is."

"One sec." Jiffy clicked on her keyboard and traced her acrylic fingernail along the computer's ancient monitor. "Ah. Good."

Leah waited expectantly for an answer. Instead, Jiffy opened up the latest issue of *Star* magazine. "Please have a seat and I'll call you when something changes."

"Hello? Shazan Ali? Room?"

"A seat, please." Jiffy gestured toward the seating area.

"Can you just tell me her room number? I won't sneak in. I swear." Leah drummed her fingers on the counter. She would definitely sneak past this redheaded bimbo the first chance she got.

"Please have a seat." Jiffy seemed to be reciting from the hospital receptionists' guidebook. "And we will call you if anything changes."

"Listen, you little minimum-wage-earning—"

"Leah, come on." Coach dragged Leah away before she could lunge over the counter and strangle the receptionist. "Getting thrown out of here won't help Shazan."

Leah settled down into an orange plastic chair and shifted this way and that. "I can't deal with this. I'm going to go look for her."

She stood up, stretched and faked toward the bathroom. "Too much water." She smiled sweetly at Jiffy. The second the receptionist looked down at her desk, Leah dashed past the desk.

"Hey!"

Leah didn't look back.

"Get back here! I'm calling security!"

Whatever. She'd been thrown out of more respectable establishments than this stupid hospital.

"Hospital security, call on line one. Security—" the loudspeaker announced.

Ugh, she hated hospitals. The stark, white walls, everyone walking around looking somber. The plasticky Jell-O smell. Leah paraded down the central hallway, but all the rooms were dark and full of machinery.

"Looking for Shazan?"

Leah whirled around.

Bill Collins. Shazan's ex-boyfriend. The reason she was here today.

"Why are you here?"

Bill ignored the question. "She was in the O.R. She's in room 202. Upstairs."

Leah hesitated. It felt like a betrayal to Shazan to accept this creep's help.

"Come on. I'll take you."

Grateful despite her annoyance, Leah followed him into the elevator. "She's going to be okay," Bill said. "She's young, strong. She'll be fine. She has to be."

"Do they, uh, know what happened?"

"It was those pills." Bill punched floor two in the elevator keypad. "She took, like, ten of them. They said she overdosed on them and that stopped her heart. I told her to stop taking them. I told her…" His voice seemed to fade.

Leah scowled. "Yeah, you also broke up with her."

"She had a real problem with those pills. She was obsessed with her weight. Every time I took her to dinner she would ask the waiter for the number of calories in her food. Then she would eat two bites and say she was full. It was nuts."

What was wrong with that? Leah frowned. First her father and now Bill. Leaving the women who loved them and tried to look their best for them.

Jackasses.

"I don't know what her problem was. She was absolutely perfect. She didn't need to lose any weight."

"You guys are really something," Leah muttered mostly to herself. "You want girls who are skinny little twigs but get pissed when they try to watch their weight."

"I loved her the way she was."

"Yeah, sure."

"I don't know why I'm having this conversation with you. You're probably her supplier." Bill punched the keypad again as if that would hurry the crawling elevator to the second floor.

"Hey." Leah turned and slammed him by the shoulders easily into the elevator wall, her anger taking over her good sense. "I had nothing to do with this. She wanted to look good in her Snow Ball dress. She wanted to look good for you!"

"Get off me!"

Leah released him as the elevator door opened.

"Crazy bitch…" she heard him mumble as the elevator door closed with him inside.

Leah ran down the hall and realized she was crying again. Why hadn't she said something to Shazan? If she had only said or done something this morning, none of them would be here today.

Room 202.

Leah stood outside the closed door, hand on the doorknob. Her mom and dad would be in there. Worried Pakistani parents who would want to know how this had happened to their beautiful, talented young daughter. And Leah had no answer.

She peeked in through the window. Shazan was lying in the bed, folded white sheet all the way up to her chin. Her eyes were closed and she wasn't moving. Her usually animated face was pasty white. Shazan's mother, head covered with a hijab, sat at Shazan's feet with her head bowed.

Leah couldn't go in. She should, but she couldn't. She turned and rushed back down to the first floor. Not now. Not while Shazan looked…like that.

Jiffy gave her a dirty look.

Leah gave her one back.

"Hey," Jay called from the seating area. "There you are. Did you see her?"

"What are you doing here?" Leah accepted his hug and watched over his shoulder as the coach got up to talk to Jiffy once again.

"I came to get you."

The words should have filled Leah with happiness, but the shock of seeing Shazan lying so still and silent in the bed had taken over her senses. "She's so... I didn't go in. Her boyfr—ex, ah, Bill is here, too. Somewhere."

"Let's get you home." Jay didn't release her from his grip. "You don't look too good. I heard about the game."

Leah pulled away. "I want to stay. I want to be here when she wakes up."

"That could be a while." Coach retook her seat next to Jay and picked up *Time* magazine. "Jiffy over there said she's had surgery. It'll take a while for the anesthesia to wear off. Another few hours before anyone can see her."

Leah hesitated. The disinfectant smell of the hospital was giving her a headache and she felt useless just sitting around. Maybe some time with Jay would clear her head.

"Come on." Jay sensed she was weakening. "Let's get some dinner and we'll come back."

Dinner. Ha. The thought of food made her want to puke.

Leah let him lead her by the hand to his Mustang. "We have to be back in an hour, okay?"

Jay drove. Leah didn't care where or how fast.

"What happened?"

"She's been stressed lately. About everything," Leah lied. She didn't want to reveal her friend's secret. Those damn pills. How could Shazan have taken so many? How could she have been so stupid? Leah thought back to her own pill ingestion. How many had she been taking every day? Three? Four? Was she in dangerous territory, too?

Jay glanced sidelong at Leah. "That's it?"

Leah didn't answer.

The wait at Red Robin was only five minutes before Leah and Jay were seated in the sunny atrium by a bubbly teenager.

Leah gazed out at the busy parking lot of the strip mall. It was almost the holiday season. She'd almost forgotten about Thanksgiving the following week.

"I'll have a mushroom-Swiss melt." Jay folded his menu. "And a vanilla malt."

Leah glanced up at the waitress. "Um. The same, I guess." Her stomach was an empty hollow and she couldn't even think of food.

"So tell me what happened at the game."

Leah folded her hands, crisscrossing her fingers over each other. Funny, today her hands looked like a stranger's. Long, slim…almost bony.

"We got a call that Shazan had passed out in the locker room. The paramedics said she'd had a heart attack," Leah said, her voice trembling. The numbness of the hospital was beginning to wear off and the reality of the situation was starting to set in. A seventeen-year-old had had a heart attack. Somehow being benched from the next basketball game seemed so small suddenly.

Jay took a sip of his water, his eyes not leaving Leah's. "How do you think this happened?"

"I don't know. I wish I did." Leah avoided his eyes. "I just—"

The food arrived. Plates piled high with juicy burgers and mounds of extra-crispy french fries. Tiny cups of ranch and barbecue sauce decorated the sides of the dishes.

"Bill broke up with her this morning. I wonder if—" Leah absently reached over to Jay's plate and took a french fry. The warm, salty potato flavor exploded in her mouth.

What the hell was she doing?

She nearly spit out the remains of the french fry onto the plate, but noticed Jay was watching her closely. She forced herself to swallow.

"Swear to me you won't take those pills anymore."

Leah blinked in surprise. "What do you mean?"

"I know about the pills. Jenn told me. Shazan bought them online from some Mexican Web site and she took, like, four a day. They sped up her heart-beat and burned calories. And did this to her. You know what I'm talking about."

"I don't—"

"Leah, don't bullshit me. I watched you go from polishing off a double cheeseburger and finishing all the fries to picking at a salad for an hour." Jay gave her a hard look. "You keep saying you're not hungry. Exactly what Shazan always says. You are not going to end up like her. I won't let you."

"I'm not taking pills." Leah stared at her still-full plate. *That* was true. She had finished off the last of them that morning. She'd been hoping to get more from Shazan after the game. And then this had happened.

"Swear?"

The silence went on much longer than Leah was comfortable with. She swallowed painfully. "Swear."

"Good." Jay picked up his fork. "Now let's finish dinner and go get a brownie sundae at Ben and Jerry's."

Leah swallowed nervously. "I'm not really hungry."

Jay raised an eyebrow.

"No, seriously."

"You are eating every bite on that plate. I've seen you do it before and you can do it now."

"Jay!"

"Just cut the crap. You have a problem. I think you might have an eating disorder."

Another one. Her mother. Coach. Now her closest friend.

Leah rolled her eyes. "Look at me. Do I look like I have an eating disorder?"

Jay looked her up and down. "Yes."

"What!"

"You've lost, what, sixty pounds in the past month and a half? That's insane."

"I've been working out."

"And not eating."

"I eat enough." Leah picked up her burger and took a tiny bite. The Swiss cheese seemed to melt away in her mouth. The perfect tinge of spicy horseradish. "See?"

"Keep going."

After another bite, Leah started to feel nervous. She set the burger down. Jay didn't seem as though he was going to let up, and her napkin was out of reach so her bite-and-spit technique wasn't going to work.

Leah finished about half the burger and most of the fries. She would get rid of it. She couldn't allow this food in her body. She would do what she did in L.A. It was the only way.

"I need to run to the restroom." Leah finished her glass of water and stood up. "I'll be back in a minute."

"No." Jay met her eyes. "You won't."

Leah blinked.

"Sit down." The sunlight hit Jay's face in a way that hardened his jaw and suddenly he looked much older than a teenager. And sounded it, too.

"What?"

"I know what you're trying to do."

"What do you think I'm going to do in there?"

"I'm not stupid, Leah. I know what you've been doing. Now, unless you want me to have a chat with the coach about your bulimia, you'll tell me exactly how it came to this."

twelve

Panic Room
150 lbs

She'd gained weight. She'd gained back two pounds and only had a week left till the *Jade* photo shoot.

Leah circled her room eyeing the newest addition, a beaten-up burgundy punching bag that she'd dragged out of the basement.

What the hell was Jay thinking, making her eat like that? He wasn't her mother. He wasn't even her boyfriend. What right did he have? He'd stuffed her stupid and left her on her doorstep.

Leah strapped on her gloves and gave the punching bag a hard thump. The only thing her father had left behind. A clunky, unwanted thing.

Like her.

Wham! That was for Jay. That was for him acting like he cared about her, only to sabotage her modeling career.

Wham! Wham! Wham!

Espresso Bean yowled in terror and ran for cover under the bed.

"Sorry, baby! I'm just *very* upset right now." *Wham, wham, wham.*

It felt great. She'd spent the day punching the hell out of the bag. Instead of going to school. Or practice.

She was too humiliated to face her teammates after being benched for next weekend's game.

And afraid. What if Jennifer had told the whole school about Shazan's pills? And how Leah was her partner in crime?

Wham! Wham! Wham! That was for Jennifer's little button nose and rosy lips.

How dare Jay accuse her of having an eating disorder? Not everyone was obsessed with their weight like his precious Jennifer Chan.

Dumb bitch had ratted her out. Now Jay didn't trust a word she said. How dare Jennifer break up a perfectly solid friendship?

Wham! Wham! Wham!

"Ouch!"

Leah dropped her arms and rubbed her right

shoulder. The shooting pain continued to travel down her arm to her wrists. She quickly unbound her hands and tried to rotate her shoulder.

"Ahh!" She couldn't help the yell.

God, what had she done? The championship game was just two weeks away. She couldn't do any damage to her throwing arm.

Ding!

A forum alert from the ANA Web site. That morning she had posted a frustrated note about the two pounds she'd managed to gain that week. Because of Jay. She had to be a hundred and forty pounds for the photo shoot. It was the only way.

Once her picture was in magazines, everyone would see. There was nothing wrong with her. She was fine. She was normal.

Leah noticed several replies to her post.

Drink only water. Yeah, right. That never worked. It just made her dizzy. She scrolled to the next one.

Exercise more. She was already running five miles a day despite her shin splints and a throbbing pain on the sides of each knee.

Sleep more so you're not awake to eat anything. Leah frowned. That wasn't bad. She could fake sick and stay in bed all week. Then no one would ask questions when she emerged ten pounds thinner by the end of the week. Stomach flu, she could claim.

Drink chicken broth. It keeps you full, people think you're eating and it has practically no calories. Dilute it with water.

Perfect. She loved this site. Chicken broth. Nothing but chicken broth this week and staying in bed.

She surfed through the pictures of thin girls on the Web site. Thinspiration, they were called. So thin, so perfect. Their slim arms, long fingers posed on slender hips. Chiseled cheekbones. Tiny thighs.

Girls like Nicole Richie and Mary-Kate Olsen pouted back at her.

They were so lucky. How did they stay so thin?

"Leah! Come downstairs please!"

"I ate already, Mama," Leah called back. Not this again. Her mother hadn't forced her to go to the doctor when Leah had insisted she was too trauma-tized after Shazan's collapse.

Silence from downstairs, and then Leah heard her mother's footsteps climbing the stairs.

God. Not now. Leah quickly logged out of the site and left her Internet Explorer window open to the high school's sports page. Varsity cheerleader rushed to hospital after cardiac arrest.

"When I call you, you come downstairs. You hear me?" Victoria entered without waiting. She froze when she saw the punching bag. "Where did that come from?"

Leah rolled her eyes and gave the bag a slight shove. Her mother hated being reminded of her father, but she didn't care. She liked seeing her mother thrown off balance. Leah couldn't help but feel that maybe she had dragged the bag into her room just for the reaction. "The basement. You knew it was there."

"I—" Victoria swallowed. "Yes, I did. Be careful. Don't—let it fall on you."

"I'm going to lie down for a while, I don't feel too good. So, talk to you later?" Leah rubbed her shoulder. Still sore.

"You coming down with something?"

"I might be," Leah lied. "I was feeling a bit feverish all day. Maybe I should stay home tomorrow."

"Sit down."

"Mama."

"Sit. Now."

Leah flopped down on the bed and closed her eyes. "I feel sick."

"Jay called four times. Are you going to call him back?"

"No."

"You cut school today." Victoria's voice reached Leah through her haze of thoughts. "And Coach Richards called me to say that you were benched for the next game, but you didn't even go to practice today. What's up with that?"

Leah flopped onto her belly and started unraveling her bedspread. "I wasn't feeling well. I told you."

"I'm rescheduling the doctor's appointment."

Not this again.

"I just need rest."

"Look. I know you're worried about Shazan, but you can't just stop going to school." Victoria tried to reach for Leah's hair, but Leah quickly pulled away. She was still losing wads of hair every day. She didn't want a repeat freak-out like in O.C. "It's the week of Thanksgiving. We're not even doing anything in school."

"You're going tomorrow. Understand? Now come down for dinner."

"Fine." Leah knew arguing wouldn't get her anywhere here.

Leah waited until her mother had closed the door behind her. She dialed the hospital again.

"Hello? I'm calling about the status of Shazan Ali. I'll hold."

Leah continued to pace and paused in front of her mirror. Her cheekbones were fat puffs. A double chin. All the fat Jay had forced her to have. How could she be in a magazine like this?

Fat. So much fat on her cheeks. She had to lose it. She had a week.

"Hello? You're calling about Shazan Ali's status?"

"Yes." Leah's heart pounded.

"I'm afraid because of privacy laws, we can't give that information out over the phone." The voice continued to speak and explain that she had to be a member of the family or come in during visiting hours to see Shazan.

She hung up the phone without saying goodbye or thank-you.

She had a very bad feeling about this.

"Leah! Dinner! Now!"

Everything was spiraling completely out of control. School, the game, her friendship with Jay, now Shazan's health.

There was just one thing she had under control.

"Mama! Do we have any chicken broth?"

145 pounds

Leah obsessively searched the ANA Web site. There had to be more tips. The girls were becoming less and less shy and were starting to post pictures of themselves.

They were all so thin. No way was Leah going to post a picture. They would laugh at her for being so fat after so much dieting.

The chicken broth diet was working. She'd already lost four pounds that week. She'd convinced Victoria she had the flu and the only thing she could keep down was plain chicken broth and Sprite Zero. Her mother had allowed her a day of bed rest and school was out for the rest of the week.

The flu symptoms weren't hard to fake because of her feverish face and harbored breathing. Leah didn't know what was really wrong with her and she didn't care. She was five pounds away from her goal.

She'd called the hospital six times that week and they wouldn't tell her anything. No one answered the phone at Shazan's house.

She'd never felt so alone.

Refresh. Refresh. She refreshed the Web site for the umpteenth time. Everyone was saying to be as dehydrated as possible to look thinner. God, she'd just finished an entire bottle of water post her five-mile run. She had to get rid of it.

She pinched her hips. So much fat. So much fat left to lose. It was the chicken broth. It probably had way more calories than she thought.

She had to throw up the chicken broth she'd drunk for dinner. And all the water.

She closed and locked the door of her bathroom and kneeled on the floor. Nothing.

She gagged.

"Try again. Try again," she chanted. She stuck a finger down her throat and waited.

Nothing.

"Come on, come on. You can do this."
She forced her finger down her throat again.
She spit up water.
She leaned her head against the toilet and cried.

thirteen

Best in Show
140 lbs

Leah couldn't stop shivering in the dressing room. She was wearing a thin robe over her underwear and was literally trembling.

The modeling shoot was in full swing at the Chateau Marmont in L.A. The *Jade* crew had taken up an entire set of suites on the top floor and girls were running in and out of the rooms, half dressed and half made-up.

Victoria had deposited Leah into a room with a chair labeled Lynnette M and a stack of *Cosmopolitan* magazines. Leah hunched down in the chair and tried to warm her cold, dry hands.

Was no one else freezing? Some blond Hollywood

starlet was sitting across from Leah looking bored and typing on her BlackJack while makeup artists worked on her face. She was wearing a sleeveless minidress and didn't look even the slightest bit frostbitten.

"Sweetie, you ready for hair?"

Leah jumped. Ken, some celebrity stylist, stood in front of her. He flicked his perfectly styled blond hair and held up a swatch of hair extensions. "We need to do something about that hair of yours."

Leah touched her scalp. She'd managed to hide her hair loss with bandanas, but apparently the hairdresser wasn't fooled.

"Come, come! Lots of work. Very little time!" Before she could blink, he tilted her head back into the sink and turned on the water.

"Have you seen Victoria anywhere?" Leah asked. Her mother had disappeared over half an hour ago and Leah was wondering if she was going through the same treatment.

"I did her hair a while ago. God, she's stunning. Isn't she stunning? That skin! I would sell my grandmother to the Middle East for that skin!"

Leah was sorry she asked.

A gentle scalp massage lulled Leah into a deep sleep. She dreamt she was floating on one of those huge rafts in a swimming pool. No one else was in sight. Just her. Alone.

She wished she could have stayed in the dream.

When she opened her eyes, Ken was gone. Instead she saw a stranger staring back at her in the mirror. The stranger looked like Beyoncé at the Oscars. She had long cascading light brown waves that tumbled over her shoulders. Her eyes were huge and almond shaped. Her cheekbones slim, her lips glossy and full.

Who was this?

Leah stood up on trembling legs and touched the mirror. How had this happened? Did she really look like this?

Gaunt fingers touched hers in the mirror.

"What do you think?" A soft voice startled Leah. She glanced in the mirror and saw Alfreddo settled into a swivel chair in the corner of the room, hands shoved into the pockets of his pin-striped pants.

How long had he been lurking there? And how had she not noticed him?

"Look at you." He stood up and started to move toward her.

"Yeah." Leah ran a hand through her hair. How much of it was hers, she couldn't even tell. The extensions were silky coils that sprang perfectly back into place.

"You are the most stunning here. By far."

Leah didn't take her eyes off her reflection and noticed Alfreddo didn't either.

The chill she'd been feeling earlier returned.

"Let's get you into wardrobe so you can choose first."

Leah hesitated. Where was Victoria? She'd thought her mother would be here with her, hovering, making sure everything was just right.

"Come on. I saw this green item that would be incredible on you. I want to see it on you before anyone else."

Leah shivered again. His eyes hadn't left the front of her robe. She pulled it tighter around her. "Let's go, then."

The wardrobe room looked like Mariah Carey's closet on MTV's *Cribs*. An entire floor of the hotel with racks and racks of dresses, hats, scarves, coats, everything. In the center of it all was a lady who was a dead ringer for Meryl Streep in *The Devil Wears Prada*.

"Who's this?" The lady peered over her stylish half-rimmed plastic frames. Stepping closer, Leah realized they had no lenses, they were just a fashion statement.

"Leah, er, Lynnette Mandeville."

"Size?"

"Four?" Leah said hopefully. Last week a four had fit her loosely. She'd never been so thin. Size-small jeans had never slid that effortlessly over her hips before.

The wardrober looked her over. "I don't think so."

Leah's heart sank. All that hard work for nothing.

They would send her home. She would be humiliated. She glanced over at Alfreddo, who was frowning.

"You're a zero or, max, a two. No way can you fit a four."

A happiness Leah had never known fluttered through her body. A *zero!*

"Try this."

The white dress was backless except for thin silver threads in a cobweblike pattern. The satin skirt flowed easily over her hips and thighs.

"It's a little big. See? You might be a double zero. We don't carry those because we don't want models that thin." The wardrober plucked at the spaghetti straps. "Let me pin you. Make sure you don't turn sideways to the cameras."

Too big. Something was too big on her.

"Please try to put on some weight, sweetheart. You don't look very healthy." The wardrober gave the gown a final tug. "I can barely keep these straps on you."

Leah picked up the train and hurried into the hallway where Alfreddo had waited while she changed.

"That's it. I'm going to buy that dress for you after this shoot. In a double zero of course."

Leah smiled at him for the first time. A double zero. If only she could show Shazan this dress. Her friend would be so proud of her. She would post a picture of herself on the ANA site tonight.

Leah slipped her feet into silvery sandals and was ushered to a black velvet room by Alfreddo.

Victoria was already there, perched on a piano. Her mouth dropped open when she saw Leah.

"Leah, please take your mother's spot on the piano. Victoria, we're going to have you sit on the bench as the pianist." Alfreddo moved next to the photographer and gave his orders.

The director, a balding man with a jaunty beret, nodded. "Oui. Excellent. Chop, chop!"

Leah felt herself glowing as the spotlight shone down on her. She noticed a tightening around Victoria's lips as her mother poised her fingers on the piano keys and pretended to play.

"Fans!" the director called.

Leah tossed her hair back as a cool breeze blew over her face. So this was what it was like. No wonder her mother loved it so much.

"Look this way, darling. Alfreddo, she's a bit too thin. We need to hide her chest bones as much as possible."

Leah glanced down. With the low neckline, she could see the outline of her ribs. Wasn't this what they wanted?

"Turn this way, Leah," Alfreddo called.

Flashbulbs popped nonstop over the course of the next hour.

Leah changed into the jade-green minidress Alfreddo had mentioned. The hem stopped at midthigh and rode up farther as she leaned against the Grecian pillar.

The fiery, tomato dress with the plunging neckline was next.

The finale was a black one-shoulder goddess gown.

She was the star of every shot, with Victoria fading into the background.

Every command the director called out began with "Leah, give me sexy. Victoria, please smile more."

It was over way too soon. As soon as the last picture was taken, Victoria left the room with a slam of the door.

I don't care, Leah thought bitterly. *Serves her right.*

Leah stood in the dressing room, still in the one-shoulder gown, unpinning the shoulder strap and the hem. A size 0 was *way* too big for her. How had this happened? Her collarbones jutted out and she could see every vein in her neck.

Finally. She'd been waiting for this day for so long.

A knock tore her eyes away from her reflection. "Come in."

"Need help?" Alfreddo closed the door behind him. "I can't stop looking at you."

Leah turned to tell him to get out. Instead, she turned around straight into his arms.

"Alfreddo, I—"

He kissed her, his tongue probing her mouth deep inside. "I'll take you to the top."

"Me?" Leah pulled away.

"You don't need riffraff hanging around like that photographer in O.C. Stick with me. Your mother is washed out. Over. You're the new Victoria."

The new Victoria? She, Leah, was more beautiful and desirable than *Victoria?* How was this even possible?

He kissed her again, harder. This time his hands slid the strap of her dress off her shoulder. "This isn't just business. We can be really good together."

"Oh." Leah's eyes opened in time to see her mother, a shocked expression on her face, as she stood silently in the corner of the room.

fourteen

U-Turn

Victoria and the car were gone by the time Leah got into the parking lot. She dropped her arms to her sides. Great, now this was going to turn into another thing to argue about at home. How she was never allowed to speak to Alfreddo again. How her modeling days were over. She was anorexic. She had a disease.

Never mind that Victoria was the one who'd dragged her into this whole thing in the first place.

Plus, Leah was stranded in the rapidly emptying parking lot of the Chateau Marmont. There was only one person she could call, but she still wasn't ready to talk to him. Jay. He hadn't even attempted to make peace after their fight last week, which really hurt.

He'd betrayed her and accused her of terrible things. How dare he be mad? If he didn't answer her call tonight, she would spring for a very expensive cab ride home. And expense it. To Alfreddo. Who'd run away like a scared little girl out of the room before Victoria said a word.

"Don't pick up. Don't pick up," Leah muttered as she dialed Jay's cell phone.

"What's the word?" Jay answered. He sounded… exactly the same. Like nothing had changed.

"I need to be picked up," Leah said hurriedly. "You busy?"

"Where are you?"

"Chateau Marmont."

"Twenty minutes." And he hung up.

How he was planning to get from Hollywood Hills to Sunset Boulevard in less than an hour on a Saturday night was beyond her. But true to his word, Jay's Mustang was in the driveway of the hotel just as Leah changed out of the black goddess gown and made it back into the lobby.

"Home, please." Leah got into the passenger side without any explanation. She must've been a sight in jeans and a baby T-shirt with her evening makeup and hair still on.

"Was this that whole modeling thing?"

"Yeah." Leah leaned forward and turned on the car

stereo. She didn't want to make idle conversation, nor recount the entire evening. She especially didn't want to talk about her "eating habits" or how much more weight she'd lost.

"How did the photo shoot go?"

Leah drummed her fingers along with Akon. "Okay."

"Where's your mom?"

"I don't know." Leah turned the volume louder, hoping he would get the hint.

As they took the Hollywood Hills exit, Jay turned down the stereo. "Why are you mad at me?"

Leah ignored him and flipped the visor down to check her reflection. Her makeup was still fresh, her skin dewy. She wished she could look like this every day.

"You look great, you know. Like one of those MTV videos. Were any of the movie stars there at the same time as you?"

"Demi Moore's daughter. She's gorgeous, looks just like Demi."

"And you look just like Victoria. You guys are like sisters."

Leah was silent. She was *better* than Victoria. She was the New Victoria. She had a real career choice here. Being beautiful and wanted for a living. She could deal with this.

"Here we are." Jay pulled into his driveway and turned off the ignition. "Look—"

Leah ignored Jay and got out of the car, a mix of relief and anger flowing through her. Victoria's car was not in the driveway and the lights in the house were all off. She hadn't known what Victoria's reaction would be. She had prepared herself for yelling and screaming. Altogether missing was not something Leah had anticipated.

"All set for the big game tomorrow?" Jay followed her up the front steps of her house.

"Yup," Leah's teeth chattered. Winter had set in early in L.A. and she had a major case of goose bumps on her arms. She thought of the Snow Ball gown that hung on the back of her closet door. She hadn't asked anyone else. And Jay certainly hadn't asked her.

"You going to the dance?" Leah asked him, unlocking the door. "With Jennifer?"

"Yeah. We're going to get a limo with a few of the girls on the squad and their boyfriends."

"Is that what you are now? A squad boyfriend?"

Jay laughed. "Nah."

Leah glanced at him. Yeah, right. "Do you want to come in?"

"I better get home. I told my mom I had to return some library books. We've got this whole thing going on at home. A puja, religious thing."

"Oh." Leah felt the same familiar pang. They actually did stuff together as a family. They had rituals and traditions. Looked as though all Leah and Victoria had was a sleazy modeling agent in common.

A guy she didn't even like. And she was pretty sure after tonight Victoria didn't either.

The only person Leah could ever imagine herself with was standing just inches away from her. Alone on her porch, looking thoughtful with his deep brown eyes and wavy hair. He smelled like winter. Like caramel apples and cider. Still, after all this, he was the only one she wanted.

She had to go for it. This was her chance.

"What?" He gazed at her face.

She kissed him. It had been building for far too long. She couldn't spend another evening flirting with him on her front stoop and spend all night wondering what it all meant.

She entwined her fingers in his thick hair and wrapped her arms around his neck. She felt his hands around her waist. Hesitant. But they were there. It was every bit as amazing as she'd been fantasizing about. He did want it. His tongue wouldn't be tangling with hers the way it was unless he wanted it, too.

She broke away from the kiss first. "Come inside. Come upstairs." She pulled him inside the house.

"Whoa." Jay gently drew back. "Leah—"

She searched his eyes, looking for a shred of

passion, desire. He had kissed her back. That had to mean something.

"I'm dating Jenn."

"So?"

"So?" He smoothed his hair. "This isn't going to happen."

"Why not?"

"Because it's not."

"What? Why not? Why not me?"

"Because you're you. I mean, we have this thing, but, no. You and I can't—"

Leah pressed her fingers together to keep from throwing a punch at him.

You're you? You're an imposter. You're a fat girl acting like you belong. "Leave."

"Oh, come on. Let's talk about this. That was a mistake. We were being stupid."

"You care about me?"

"Of course."

"Love me, even?"

"Yes, I do."

"Then why was that a mistake?"

"It didn't mean anything! You don't feel that way toward me, right? I know you don't. We're just friends."

Friends? He was unwilling to explore this sizzling, alive thing between them because he needed a buddy to trade lines and basketball shots with?

Leah shoved him. Hard. She was still stronger, despite all the weight she had lost, and he fell a few steps back.

"Hey."

"Get out. Just get out of my house."

"I am not leaving, until—"

"Why her? Why Jennifer? All she cares about is how she looks, how thin she is, how pretty she is. She doesn't challenge you!"

"She's not like that—"

"Yeah, she is! She's vain and selfish and stupid. She is *obsessed* with being thin."

"No, Leah." Jay stepped forward and lifted her chin, his fingers mingling with the tears flowing down her cheeks. "Jennifer is not the one with the problem. You are."

"Jay!"

"I don't think you and I should see each other for a while. I think you should get some help. I don't want you to end up like Shazan."

"I'm *not* her."

"You will be soon."

He closed the door behind him as he left.

fifteen

Eyes Wide Shut

"wake up."

No response from the still figure on the bed. Shazan's eyes remained closed even as Leah paced her room. She'd been pacing for five minutes and still no response.

"Wake up. Wake up." Leah kneeled next to the bed and laid her hand on Shazan's flat stomach. "I need to talk to you right now. C'mon, babe. Wake up!"

"Who is that?" Shazan's voice was weak, and unfamiliar, but it was her.

Leah fell onto the bed, practically crushing Shazan. "Do you know how worried people are about you? Everyone at school is asking about you."

"How did you get in here?"

"Girl, you think that whiny little Jiffy can keep me out? I don't think so." Overjoyed, Leah snapped on the bedside light. She'd left it off since she'd snuck into the room, way before visiting hours.

"What's happened to you?"

"What do you mean?" Leah touched her cheekbones. She knew Shazan would notice how much weight she'd lost. How great she must look.

"Are you sick?"

"No! Why?"

"Your face. God, look at your fingers!" Shazan stared at Leah's fingers entwined with her own.

Leah snatched her hand away. *Not you, too. Jealous.* Even Shazan was jealous.

"I did the modeling thing, remember? The photographer said I have a real future."

"What about basketball?"

"What about it?"

"How's the team? We gonna win the finals?"

"You bet." Leah grinned. "The game is in three hours, but I had to see you."

"Come back and tell me how it goes. You know, no one else has come by." Shazan rested her head back into the mound of pillows and groaned.

"Bill has. I saw him the first day."

Shazan turned her head. "He says I have a real problem."

"Ignore him."

"I think I do. I was completely addicted to those pills."

Leah took her hand again, being careful to hide her fingers from Shazan. "It's over now. Don't think about it. You'll be home soon."

Shazan smiled weakly. "You look really tired. Take a nap before the game. And come tell me how it went. I can't believe I'm missing it."

Leah hugged her. "I promise to come back here tonight and tell you all about it. Get some rest."

"Where have you been?" Allison Taylor shrieked as Leah entered the girls' locker room. "Coach is going to flip! You missed practice!"

Leah ignored her and started shuffling in place. Back and forth. Back and forth. Her shins were feeling much better, but she was just so tired. She felt as if she could fall asleep on her feet. And the room seemed to be spinning. She wished Allison would just shut the hell up.

"Hello?"

Leah turned around and snapped, "Just shut up, okay? What do you want?"

"Nothing. Jeez." Allison stopped pulling her hair into a ponytail in midair. "What's with you? Low blood sugar?"

"Bitch," Leah muttered, resuming her shuffling.

"What did you say?" Allison stepped into Leah's shuffle line. "What did you just say to me?"

"Nothing." Leah rolled her eyes. "I have a game to win, if you remember. Get the—"

"With that attitude, no wonder everyone thinks you're crazy." Allison smirked.

"You got something to say to me?" Leah rested a hand on her hip and took a threatening step forward.

Allison took it all in and laughed. "Please. The Ghetto Superstar routine isn't going to fly just because you're Miss Thang now. Warm up and get on the court."

Leah was the last one on the court, and the coach pointedly ignored her during their final huddle.

"Okay, girls. This is it. Let's make history, huh? The scout from Cal is here. He's in the third row."

Scout!

Leah glanced into the stands. Victoria was there. Front row, center. She sat alone, hands entwined, frowning. Leah looked past her. Where was the scout?

The cheerleaders took their place and Leah heard a familiar yell.

"Hey, wait up!" Jay jogged toward the court.

Leah broke into a smile. He came! He was there for her.

Instead of running toward her, Jay stopped at the

cheerleaders and grabbed Jennifer. He dipped his head and kissed her. On the lips. In front of everyone. A cheer rose from the crowd.

As he stood up, Jay's eyes met Leah's. He held her gaze and turned away as if he didn't even know her.

Leah's cheeks burned. Point taken.

East L.A. and Sonoma lined up. Leah gazed at her opponents. She could take them. Easily. This was going to be so easy.

She would have good news for Shazan tonight.

The ref blew the whistle and instantly, Leah grabbed the basketball and started dribbling toward the other basket.

"Leah, you sure you're all right? You don't look too—" Leah heard the coach's voice.

"I gotta win this one, Coach. Don't worr—" Leah raised the basketball in the air and gasped. What were those twigs that were holding up the ball? Where were her powerful, muscular arms? These looked like a scarecrow's arms. The ball was just so heavy. She dropped it and instantly it was stolen by the other team's star forward.

No chance. She was going to win this game.

She leaped into the air to block the shot.

That's when everything started to spin.

She hit the floor on her side.

And heard a crack.

"Stop!" Leah yelled as loudly as she could. "Time-out!"

"Leah!" Her mother's voice sounded very far away.

Everything continued. Just like in the locker room. Leah reached out for something to hold on to, but all she caught was thin air.

Her eyes closed and she felt herself falling.

sixteen

Fracture

тhе game.

Beep.

The game. Where was she? They had a game to play.

Passed out on the court.

Looked dizzy.

Losing her…

Eating disorder.

Were those voices real?

Leah wanted to yell out that she was fine. Everything was going to be okay. They had a game to win. They had to let her wake up.

"Aggg." She made a gurgling sound in her throat that didn't sound like anything to her ears.

* * *

She opened her eyes and saw a bright white light. No! Was she dead? Was this the white light?

"There she is." The light was gone. "Leah?"

Leah blinked. "What the hell was that? Am I dead? Is this heaven? What is that smell?"

She heard a scraping noise from the corner of the room. "You're back." Victoria was by her side in an instant. "Thank God. Thank God."

"Mama!" Leah started to cry. "What happened? Why am I here? I'm supposed to be playing the game right now. Did we lose?"

"Listen."

Leah felt something heavy around her middle. She couldn't turn onto her back. "Mama!"

"You broke two ribs."

"What?" Leah attempted to sit up, but it hurt too much to even breathe.

"You fell on the court and shattered two ribs. You had surgery yesterday."

"But the game? What happened to the game? There was a scout—"

"Game's over. You lost. Get over it."

Leah swiveled her head. Who was that? A man in the corner of the room was writing in a chart. He certainly didn't have the bedside manner to be a doctor.

"Mama?"

"We'll talk about it later. Right now we need to get you better."

"Victoria, don't coddle her. You're part of the problem."

"Hey! You got something to say to me, you say it to me. Leave my mama outta this—" Leah indignantly placed her elbows underneath her and tried to prop herself on them. Failing, she fell back into the pillow. Her arms just felt so weak. And this heavy cast—how was she going to play with this cast?

"You are a very sick young lady. We need to talk a bit about what you've done to yourself," the man said, pulling his chair up next to her. "Listen and listen well. I'm Dr. Brendan. Eating-disorder psychologist. You know you're in L.A. when there are more eating-disorder specialists than brain surgeons."

"I'm fine." Leah closed her eyes. Her lids felt so heavy. And she was so cold. "Can someone turn up the heat?"

"You've lost so much body fat so quickly that your body isn't able to adjust. That's why you're so cold." The annoying Dr. Brendan continued talking. "Keep your eyes open. If you sleep again, you might not wake up."

"That's crap." Leah forced open her eyes to see him up close. In other circumstances, she would have found him hot, but his sapphire eyes were narrowed with disapproval. Doctors were supposed to be hot and understanding and nice, like the ones on *Grey's Anatomy.* This one was just rude. She wanted a trade.

"It's not crap. You're losing hair and your nails are breaking. Your bones are as brittle as a fifty-year-old's. Your body is shutting down. Look at this." He held up her wrist. It hung limply, every bone and vein visible through the transparent skin. "This is a dying body."

"I'm fine. I just need to go home."

"The E.R. staff put food into you through an IV for the past two days. Do you understand me? You're awake because your body got the nourishment it needed. You would have died if they hadn't force-fed you."

Food? They were force-feeding her?

"You need treatment. You need to eat. You are not leaving here till we do something about your anorexia. And if I'm not mistaken, by this report of your stomach lining, you're bulimic, too."

Victoria gasped.

"There is nothing wrong with me!"

"When you start eating on your own, you get to make decisions. Until then, you are going to stay in this room. In that bed. You do not leave the room. You don't even get your shoes or clothes until you start eating again."

Leah eyed him. She was going to wear this paper gown until she downed a cheeseburger? What kind of stupidity was this? There was nothing wrong with her!

Why wasn't her mother speaking up for her? Why wasn't she telling them what a hit she'd been at the modeling shoot? How everyone loved her.

"We're going to talk every day. You are going to tell me what you've eaten and how you felt. I'm not going to let you turn into your friend Shazan."

"You're insane." Leah attempted to sit up again. Barely succeeded. "Everything's fine, okay. Shazan's going to be okay. She opened her eyes. We talked. She's going to go home soon."

"Leah." Victoria squeezed her left hand while Dr. Brendan pinched her right.

"Ouch! Quit pinching me!"

"At least you can feel that. Listen to me and listen well. You need to get better. I am not going to release you until you're eating normally again. If that means you stay here for a year, so be it. No friends. No school dances. Certainly no sports. You want that?"

"Stop trying to scare me! There is nothing wrong with me! Look at me. I was in a modeling shoot on Friday. I look great! Everyone says so." Leah touched her cheekbones. Sharp, clean bones.

"Damn photographers," Dr. Brendan muttered. "I hate this town. Look, about your friend Shazan."

"I want to see her. I promised I'd tell her how the game went."

"Shazan's gone," Victoria answered for the doctor.

"Home already? She didn't say goodbye." Leah frowned. That didn't sound like her at all. Shazan would have been here by her side, whispering conspiratorially about how they were going to get out of here, go shopping and get revenge on their ex-loves. She wouldn't just leave. Especially if she knew Leah was trapped here with Dr. McNutty.

"Leah, listen—" Victoria glanced at the doctor.

"She died early this evening. She had another heart attack. In two weeks, that will be you."

seventeen

Mommy Dearest

Leah stared at the macaroni and cheese perched on the edge of her bed. She was not putting that into her body. Not a chance.

Dr. Brendan and Victoria had finally left.

And here she was alone. White padded room. Bed. Socks. Hospital gown. That was it.

Shazan dead? No way. Her friend was going to be an Abercrombie model. She had her whole life ahead of her. They were lying to her. They had to be. Just to scare her. The second she got out of here she would call her friend and they would laugh about this whole stupid incident.

Leah touched the heavy cast. Apparently in a week, they would remove it and just tape the ribs.

The break had been bad apparently. The on-call doctor had explained that her bones were brittle from the lack of calcium in her diet and she'd lost most of the fat and muscle in her rib cage, leaving her ribs vulnerable.

Everything had fallen apart so quickly.

They'd lost the game. And the finals. All because of her.

She'd kissed Jay, thinking, yes, this time it was going to happen.

And it hadn't. He hadn't even come to see her yet.

She needed a plan. She had to get her life back. Finally, everything was in place. She was thin. She was on the cover of *Jade* magazine. She could finally be one of the girls she'd envied for so long.

She had to get out of here and away from the crazy doctor and his mac and cheese.

As much as she tried to ignore it, the smell wafted to where she was propped up on three pillows. Rich and creamy. She could practically taste the cheese. And the pasta. She hadn't touched pasta in months.

Leah turned away. Not a bite.

Dr. Brendan was *not* going to blackmail her into eating. She might as well take the fat and inject it into her veins. She'd be back to being two hundred pounds in a week if she did that.

A knock at the door woke her from her stupor.

"You're sitting up." Victoria closed the door behind her.

"If I don't breathe too hard, it doesn't hurt." Leah attempted a smile.

"I've never seen you black out before. The whole gym just froze. And Sonoma forfeited the game."

Leah felt a sinking in her stomach. All because of her. Could she ever show her face again? "What did Coach say?"

"Just to get better, babe." Victoria sat at the edge of the bed, moving the plate of mac and cheese closer to Leah. "Did you understand what the doctor said? He won't let you out of here until you're well."

"Mama, come on! You see me. I'm *fine*. I was just dehydrated that day."

"You are not fine."

"Mama!"

"I told you before. I saw the signs…but I let you get away with it. I wanted us to be in that damn photo shoot so badly I was willing to sacrifice your health."

Victoria pressed her palms to her temples. "I should have checked you in here myself when I found those pills. I should have called Shazan's mom. If I had, I wouldn't have had to go to her funeral today."

Leah stared dully at Victoria. It couldn't be true. Shazan. Full-of-life, beautiful Shazan. The only one that understood.

"Her parents are falling apart. Her mother kept begging her to wake up. Kept telling her all her friends were there to see her and she needed to wake up." Victoria wiped away a tear. "That could have happened to you if your body hadn't shut down at the game."

"I don't believe you. She can't be gone—"

"She's *dead,* Leah. You hear me? Dead." Victoria took a folded piece of paper out of her purse and threw it on Leah's lap.

Leah unfolded the newspaper page. Sonoma High School Cheerleader Dies of Drug Overdose. Funeral to Be Held December 8th.

She silently read the rest of the article.

She's really gone.

Leah felt her breath catch. "Oh, Mama—"

"Don't Mama me. You need to listen to me. Back in the eighties, this disease wasn't known. Back then, if a girl lost that much weight, people would just say, 'eat and you'll be fine.' I had no one. I had to make the decision that I wanted to live. For myself. For you." Victoria sighed. "Now there are drugs, treatments, counseling. We'll get you everything you need. But we will fix you."

"I don't need any of that. I can fix this on my own. I was just dehydrated. That's all."

"Why are you not touching this food?"

Leah didn't answer. She crumpled the newspaper in her hand. *In two weeks, that will be you.*

She couldn't get the doctor's words out of her head. Two weeks.

"I shouldn't have pressured you into modeling. You were such a perfect little girl. So strong. An amazing future ahead of you. I ruined it. I ruined you."

Leah stared at her mother, who sobbed uncontrollably. Seeing Victoria lose it like that unnerved her. Was her body really falling apart like that? Was there a chance that she might...die?

"I'm scared," she said, almost to herself.

"We'll get through this. We will. You will get strong. You will play ball for the Bruins."

"The modeling? Mama, I'm on the cover—"

"I thought that if you were a successful model without any eating disorders, I would be able to redeem myself. It would mean I wasn't a screwup. I wanted you to become a successful version of me. But I almost killed you."

"Mama, it wasn't your fault. I did this—" Leah gestured towards her ribs "—to myself. No one forced me."

Victoria picked up the bowl of mac and cheese. "And no one is going to force you to get well either. You need to decide for yourself."

Leah stared down at her bare legs and stockinged

feet. Those weren't her legs. Those legs would never take her to UCLA to play for the Bruins. "I want to get better."

Leah opened her mouth and allowed Victoria to place a forkful of macaroni in it.

eighteen

The Basketball Diaries

Leah gazed out at the snowflakes dancing outside her windows. She'd been moved out of the psychiatric wing and into a normal room after she'd started eating on her own.

She even had her own clothes back and her mother even had snuck in Espresso Bean for a visit. The purring cat did more for Leah's sadness than anything else. Victoria had promised to bring Beanie back later in the week.

Leah blinked as a snowball hit her window. Wow. Snow in L.A. And early in December at that. Fitting that tonight was the Snow Ball. Shazan would have loved it.

Tears filled her eyes. Nothing would bring her friend back now. She'd never felt so much guilt and remorse. She thought back to the last conversation she and Shazan had had.

I'll get better, I swear.

Knock, knock.

Leah didn't lift her head from the pillow. Jay, the basketball team and the cheerleaders had come to see her in the past month, but the visits had started to taper off. For the past few days, no one had come by. Except for Victoria, who never left except to get coffee and changes of clothes. Leah didn't expect anyone except candy stripers anymore.

Jay's head appeared followed by an enormous gift basket. "'We're not shy, Wednesday! We're contagious!'"

Addams Family reference. Leah was in no mood to play.

"Hey." Leah swiped at her cheek with the back of her hand, surprised. "What are you doing here?" She observed Jay's suit. Black suit, black tie. He looked like a Mafia man. Sexy.

"I was on my way to pick up Jenn for the Snow Ball. I wanted to see you first, though. How's my tie?"

"Terrible. You're such a loser," Leah deadpanned.

"I've missed you," Jay said simply, setting the

basket down next to Leah. She eyed it. Chocolate bars, peanuts, fruit. All her favorites. "The team sent this. They said to forget about the game and just get better. They need you to kick some real ass next year."

"I will." Leah reached for the basket. "Hand me that Snickers bar, will ya?"

"You look great." He handed her the bar, their hands touching. "Much better than last week."

Leah pulled her hand away first. "I'm eating on my own. I can't believe I gave up chocolate." She bit into the chocolatey peanuty goodness. "Heaven."

"Listen, about what happened—"

Leah shrugged. "I don't want to talk about it."

"I didn't think you would. You're a great girl, but you know—"

"I get it, we're friends." She pointedly gestured toward her knee, where his hand was resting.

He removed it quickly.

She didn't get it. But it wasn't going to happen and she wasn't going to lose any more dignity trying. Maybe she would never get over Jay. But she was tired of letting him walk all over her. There was someone out there for her. Someone who loved her for her.

"Yeah." Jay looked visibly relieved. "So, we're, uh, okay?"

"Definitely. I have plenty of other things to worry

about. The game. College. Doing something in Shazan's memory. I don't really have time to obsess over you, if you're worried about that."

He laughed. Uneasily.

"Cool. By the way, there's some guy in the hall. Says he met you in O.C."

Leah's head pounded. "Tall, light hair? Tan?"

"Yeah."

"Let him in." She crumpled up the Snickers wrapper. "I know him."

"Okay," Jay said doubtfully. He went to the door and stuck his head out. "Hey! You can come in."

Cillian appeared, arms full of flowers. Tan and gorgeous as ever. "I hope it's okay I'm here. Your mom said—"

"What are you doing here?" Leah scowled at him. Last time she'd seen him, he was pawing at her mother's model friend.

"I saw this." Cillian laid an advance copy of *Jade* magazine onto Leah's lap. "And I knew something was wrong. When I asked Alfreddo, he said you were in the hospital."

Leah glanced down at the magazine. She was on the cover! But she looked so strange. All angles and light. That wasn't her face. Where were her lush eyelashes and flushed cheeks? This girl had dead eyes and razored cheekbones. She looked…old! Much older than herself. And tired. She didn't look like that in real life. Did she?

"You were so beautiful in O.C. What happened to you? Why did you do this?"

"Because you wanted it."

"I did not!"

"I was an idiot. I was trying to be something I wasn't."

Cillian laid a hand on hers. "I'm sorry. What happened? How did you end up here?"

"I fainted. After not eating for two days."

"Damn."

"Yeah. Pretty much."

All three were silent for a second. The question in Jay's eyes was obvious.

"Cillian, Jay. Jay, Cillian."

They eyed each other.

"Cillian is an up-and-coming photographer for Mom's agency. Jay's my neighbor."

They grunted at each other.

Cillian scooted closer to Leah. Jay stepped closer to hear what he was saying.

"You are perfect the way you are." Cillian lightly touched her cheek. "Alfreddo told me he would have my job if he caught me with you again. I had to stay away."

"What? Why didn't you say something? I thought you and Paula—"

"No way." Cillian lowered his voice further. "I wanted to call you so many times, but I thought—"

"But you didn't," Leah reminded him. "What about Alfreddo now? Why aren't you quaking in your boots? Won't he find out about this visit?"

"I don't give a damn about Alfreddo anymore. I should have told you in the first place. He's such a jackass. Your mom fired him, you know that?"

Leah laughed. "Thank God. He was such a creep."

Jay cleared his throat. "Leah. I'm going to go."

"Okay." Leah barely glanced up. He hesitated in the doorway, not looking like he was in any hurry to get to his precious Jennifer.

"Give me a second chance?" Cillian asked. That easy grin of his was obviously not used to hearing the word *no.* "We were pretty good together."

Leah glanced from him to Jay to the flowers all her friends had brought her. The Bruins jersey the coach had sent her.

The magazine Cillian had brought. Who was that stranger staring back at her? Who were those girls on the ANA Web site? That wasn't her life. Her life was going to begin in this room.

"We'll see. Like I told Jay," Leah said, slyly gazing

from Jay to Cillian, "I have a lot of other things to look forward to right now. I have my whole life ahead of me. But for right now, could one of you hand me that Milky Way bar? I'm starving!"

Dear Kimani TRU Reader,

We hoped you enjoyed *Shrink to Fit* by Dona Sarkar. If you're new to TRU and would like to read more stories like this one, pick up a copy of *How to Salsa in a Sari* published earlier this year. What follows is an excerpt from *How to Salsa in a Sari*.

one

Life's Tough. Get a Helmet!

"**Your** life is going to change forever tonight, so be ready."

Issa Mazumder stopped in her tracks at her mother's mystifying phrase. "Mom!" she protested. Still clad in Powerpuff Girl pajamas, not to mention sans coffee, Issa was in no shape for guessing games. "You are not messing with me right now!"

"I won't say another word. I was going to wait till the weekend, but today seems like a good day. It's a surprise."

Issa dropped into the chair opposite her mother and prepared her best wide-eyed "look how cute I am" expression. Nothing she loved more than one of Alisha Mazumder's surprises.

Just last month she and Alisha had made an impromptu trip to Manhattan when the Cirque du Soleil had come to the city. They had worked as ushers and seen the show for free from the front row.

"I'll die! I'm not even kidding. Physically die!"

"I'll pick you up here at six. Be ready!" Alisha Mazumder raised an eyebrow over a steaming coconut latte. "I don't think you'll physically die."

"I can't think of anything else now. How could you do this to me?"

"This is quite the change from the panic-stricken daughter who was totally freaking last night about some exam." Alisha laughed. "What happened to 'oh my God, I'm totally going to fail the World Politics midterm. My life means nothing beyond this exam!'"

"Whatever. I'm never panicked. Steady as a train. See that?" Issa flexed her puny biceps. "And quit changing the subject."

"Steady like a train wreck." Alisha grinned. "Talked to Adam finally?"

"Yup." Issa had to smile. She supposed the subject could turn to Adam. For a few seconds anyway.

Anxious, adorable Adam. Her boyfriend of two years had called at midnight with a panic attack of his own. He needed help. He needed support. More than anything…he needed her notes.

And if anything could make Issa feel better, it was fixing a problem. She'd drilled the study material into Adam's head and realized that she knew her stuff pretty well in comparison to her first and only love.

"He hadn't studied for the exam at all. His ass was set up to fail," Issa said as she got up to fill a mug with soy milk and pop it into the microwave. The Mazumder family ritual of spending a half hour every morning discussing school, work, cute boys, et cetera, over coconut lattes was Issa's favorite part of the day. Often, she felt it was the only time she and her mother could completely and totally be themselves, fuzzy pajamas and bed-head included. Over the years, she come to savor these last few minutes of dreamy innocence before the Mazumder girls donned protective shields and journeyed into the perilous world of high school.

"So, if Adam wasn't studying, what was Nerd Boy doing all weekend?" Alisha folded a corner in her *Modern Art and Design* magazine, buffed nails gleaming as she flipped the pages. "Shooting up? Loose women, fast cars?"

"Ha-ha." Issa made a face. She retrieved the steaming mug of milk from the microwave after the insistent beep. "He was sick, remember? He called me yesterday and told me he was on bed rest all day Friday and Saturday. Do you need to be calling him Nerd Boy all the time?"

"Uh, yeah. Otherwise, why would he date you?" Alisha teased, swirling her coffee cup. "Nerd Girl!"

"Hey!" Issa glanced up from where she was adding coconut syrup and two shots of espresso into her monster-size latte. "I protest!"

"Mommy, Mommy, I'm going to fail school. Will you still love me? Will you support me if I don't get into any colleges and have to live in a two-story cardboard box on the driveway?" Alisha mimicked Issa's paranoid ramblings from last night. "I swear, if I'd studied half as much as you do I would have been the mayor by now."

"You could be a rocket scientist, Mama." Alisha was an enigma to Issa. An eternally glamorous, bohemian version of Catherine Zeta-Jones, Alisha looked ten years younger than her thirty-six years, and was one of the most dynamic people Issa knew. Everyone who met Alisha was in love with her wit, charm and vivacious personality within ten minutes.

"Thanks for your concern, my love." Alisha stood and shook the cheese Danish crumbs off her tiered blue velvet skirt. "You need a ride to school?"

Issa had to call Adam one last time to make sure he wasn't panicking, but refused to confess that to her mother and risk more teasing. "I'll walk, actually. Clear my head. Make sure I have all the world policies straight."

"Again, I repeat. Nerd!" Alisha called as she waltzed up the stairs. "Where do you get it from?"

Issa caught sight of Alisha's half-empty mug on the kitchen counter and almost laughed.

A total free spirit. No rules and regulations could keep Alisha in one place for long. While Issa envied Alisha's daydreamy attitude, she knew that one person in the house had to be somewhat responsible.

"I wonder, too, Mama," Issa murmured, smiling as she rinsed out the cup and placed it into the dish-washer. Sometimes she swore her list-making obses-sion and punctuality existed to compensate for Alisha's short-term memory. Speaking of short-term memory, Alisha had managed to escape without re-vealing her surprise.

"Damn. She's good. She's really good," Issa grum-bled as she grabbed a notepad off the kitchen counter. So much to do today.

One, drop off article at *Apex*.

She wrote for the school newspaper as part of her writing scholarship at the prestigious private school. She worked hard on all her articles for the *Athens Apex* knowing Alisha would never be able to afford to send her to the hoity-toity school without the scholarship.

Last night, Issa had just finished up an investigative article on Thomas Calabran, one of the reclusive oil tycoons in town, three days before the deadline. Even she had to admit the article was one of her better works.

"Hey, your aunt Helen called." Alisha yelled over the sound of her hair dryer upstairs. "She wants to know if you want to do Kwanzaa in Atlanta again this year. Call her back, would you?"

Strict Aunt Helena. Her father's oldest sister never had approved of the mixed-race marriage of her Indian mother and African-American father. But she loved Issa like her own child and insisted Issa "keep her black flavor ripe." Issa had celebrated the African holiday during the last week of December with her father's family every year since she was a kid. Despite her father's absentee status, it was the one holiday she looked forward to, just to be able to see her extended family. The black, red and green decorations, the homegrown fruits, beautiful objects of art…she loved it all. The weeklong celebration made her feel like a part of her father's culture. A part she felt like she barely got to experience in the preppy, white-bread Connecticut town they had moved to at the beginning of high school.

"I'll call her, Mom. Please just finish doing your hair. You don't want to frizz."

"Aye-aye, Capitane."

Issa smiled and returned to her list.

Two, talk to Professor Kidlinger about independent study project.

English was the class she excelled at without trying and her teacher Ms. Kidlinger was always telling her she would accomplish great things with her talent for words. Issa had come up with a master plan to ask her teacher if she could do an independent study project on Jane Austen and her life during the *Pride and Prejudice* era next semester.

Three...

"Hey!" Alisha called again, snapping Issa out of her list. "Cute boy on the patio alert!"

Issa's pen hit the counter a second before the knock on the kitchen door. "Are those cheese Danishes I smell?"

Adam.

"Hey!" Issa threw open the door and greeted the smiling junior with a big kiss. "I didn't expect to see you this morning."

Her Adam. Buttery ribbons of blond hair, eyes that twinkled like Christmas lights and the most innocent smile Issa had ever seen. So he wasn't traditionally gorgeous with his mild sprinkling of acne and too-thin frame, but Issa found him adorable and perfect for her.

Adam's lightly freckled face crinkled even more around the eyes than usual. "Hello, gorgeous."

Issa's cheeks burned. Adam always claimed she looked like the girl from Bend It Like Beckham, but she didn't believe it for a second. Alisha was the great beauty in the family, Issa was just a mess of tangled, murky brown hair and tennis-ball-size, anxious eyes. Their homecoming pictures had been beautiful, though, his cream complementing her cocoa.

"How're you feeling? Better?" Issa stuffed a Danish into his hand.

"Listen, I need to run to an early-morning Science Club meeting, but I wanted to bring you this." From behind his back appeared a single lavender rose, Issa's favorite. "Thanks so much for helping me last night."

"You didn't have to." Issa took the flower and inhaled.

"I did have to," Adam said, encircling his hands around her back, pulling her head under his chin. Issa breathed in his CK aftershave as she leaned on him.

"Thanks so much, Iz. You're amazing." He kissed her nose. "Now I really need to go. I'll see you in class."

"Love you!" Issa called to him as he jogged down the driveway. He held up an arm without turning around.

She smiled and twirled on her bare feet. Adam was happy again. Problem solved.

* * *

After the last period of the day, World Politics exam successfully behind her, Issa left the school newspaper office where her article was safely nesting in the editor's layout box. She sped through the halls, having gotten a text message from Gigi five minutes earlier.

EMERGENCY! I NEED TO SEE YOU! CHEM LAB! NOW!

Issa flew around a corner and skidded on the freshly waxed floor, her Sketchers screeching to a stop.

Latina Barbie and the Skipper twins, combined weight and IQ of one hundred, stood blocking the hallway.

"Well, well." Cat Morena, aka Latina Barbie, crossed her arms, a smirk in her slanted green eyes. "If it isn't the affirmative-action case." She emphasized the word with an extra-pronounced *S* at the end. She covered her slight Cuban accent with a faux British one. "Off to help Mummy scrub the floors to earn your keep?"

Issa clenched her teeth. Rudeness on a daily basis was expected from Cat, but she was dissing Alisha now, the best art teacher Athens Academy had ever had. How low could Cat really go?

However, Issa kept quiet. She'd learned long ago that Cat *wanted* her to fight back. A cross between a dark-haired Paris Hilton and an even darker poisonous viper, Cat liked nothing better than to put one of her enemies in their place. Issa remembered well the first time she had challenged Cat. The first and last time she'd crossed Cat Morena.

"I got somewhere to be," Issa muttered, rubbing her toe against the sparkling floor.

"So, what do you want us to do about it, huh, *chica?*"

Issa could see the reflections on the floor of Cat and her entourage as Cat tossed her perfectly highlighted caramel-colored hair and smiled snidely, waiting for some sort of retort from Issa.

"No answer? Are you going to run to Mummy and tell her we're being mean to you? Are you going to cry?" Cat's singsong voice could cut sharper than any knife. "Are you wishing we would leave you alone?"

For a moment, Issa felt like she might actually cry. She didn't understand why Cat was so mean. So they'd had a fight over two years ago. She had no idea how Cat could hold a grudge for so long. How a privileged sixteen-year-old girl could be so deliberately cruel to someone was beyond Issa.

"I don't have time for this bullshit right here," Issa finally snapped, her voice betraying her bravado with a quaver. Damn it. Issa never liked giving Cat the satisfaction of knowing how to get to her. Like a vampire feeding off blood, Cat fed off people's weaknesses.

One of the blond Skipper twins, Jewel Taylor, giggled. "Aw, how cute. She's using her black talk. What's it called, Sunshine?"

"Ebonics! That's what it's called!" The other twin, Sunshine Harris, joined in the giggling,

Issa's cheeks burned. As one of the few biracial students in the school, she made sure to avoid sounding "black" for just this reason. Anything that wasn't "like, oh my God," was "black talk" to the masses of rich white folks. Even her school-teacher father would *never* have stood for Ebonics in his house.

Cat stopped laughing, an unpredictable look in her eyes. "Fine. Go," she said quietly. "Your day's about to get a whole lot worse, *chica*."

Shit.

A needle of fear jabbed Issa as she ran through the hallways. Cat hadn't spent as much time torturing her as usual. As Issa well knew, that was never a good thing. She had learned that lesson the first semester of her freshman year.

Issa had made it a point to avoid Cat at all costs for the next year and a half. And succeeded. She and Cat traveled in totally different circles. Cat was always surrounded by her perfumed, feathered, rich friends and Issa hung with down-to-earth, out-of-place types.

Only a few months ago had Cat come back into Issa's life, now that they were both enrolled for the same English class. Issa made it a point to sit in the far back of the room, huddled into oversize sweat-shirts in the corner, trying to be as invisible as possible.

Issa shivered, remembering Cat's words. By the time she reached the chemistry lab, she had a very bad case of dread squeezing at her stomach.

"Gigi! What's the emergency, girl?" Issa spotted her friend hunched over an array of tubes and beakers.

Gigi O'Neil held up a test tube filled with a suspiciously slimy green liquid. "Does this look right? Mr. Jonas said if I don't finish this lab by the end of the day, I'm totally failing the class."

"Gigi—"

"I think I just made a bomb!"

"Gigi!"

"Wait, let me put the bomb down. I don't want to blow us up before you hear the news."

Gigi set her bomb carefully into a beaker. She nervously pushed her goggles to the top of her wavy red hair and blinked her aquamarine eyes. "Just so you know, I could be wrong. If I'm right, I don't want you to hate me. I just thought you should know. Okay? So promise not to hate me?"

Issa restrained the urge to reach out and wrap her

hands around Gigi's throat. It figured, her friend had to be a ditz at a moment like this.

"Girl, do not mess with me right now!" Issa snapped, curiosity building to the point of annoyance. Even though Gigi was often theatrical, this didn't sound like the usual round of stupid Monday-morning gossip.

"So, remember you said Adam was sick on Friday night and that was why he couldn't come see the movie with us and Ishaan?"

Issa nodded.

"There you guys are." Ishaan Banerjee stormed the door of the lab, his handsome face not looking the least bit pleased. His heavy black eyebrows were drawn together in a fierce V and his usually full mouth was set in a horizontal line. "Gigi, did you tell her? I swear, I'm gonna kill that guy."

His fists were clenched and he looked ready to do some damage.

Ishaan was intense and passionate, but hardly violent. Something had brought out his protective edge. Issa wished someone would just tell her what the hell was going on. How was she always the last to know the news?

"Guys. What's going on?" Issa looked at her two closest friends. They each hesitated as they exchanged a look. "Is it that bad? Am I being kicked out of school?"

"Well," Gigi started, "Matt told Ishaan he saw Adam at Cat Morena's house on Friday night. For one of her hot-tub parties."

Issa's breath caught. Adam? No way. That was stupid. He'd been even sweeter than usual this morning. Adam would never do anything like this. He loved her and thought Cat and her friends were useless flakes.

"Future barefoot and pregnant housewives, Issa, that's all they are," he always said to her. "They're jealous of you and your real future."

This had to be some stupid rumor. Maybe there was someone who looked like Adam making the rounds. There had to be some other explanation.

Issa breathed a sigh of relief. Jeez, she expected these theatrics from Gigi, but Ishaan? He never repeated news from the Athens Gossip Mill.

That is, unless he knew it to be true.

No, not possible.

"I don't think so, guys. I mean, we know Adam. I think we're all just overreacting." She forced a smile for her friends. What if it *was* true?

"That's not the worst part." Ishaan cut her off. "Iz, *apparently* Adam was doing Jell-O shots off Cat Morena's neck."

"*What!*"

Suddenly Cat's words came back to Issa.

Your day's about to get a whole lot worse, chica.

This had to be what that horrible witch had meant.

"She's hyperventilating. Get a chair," Gigi ordered Ishaan.

"I am not—" Before she knew what was happening, Ishaan had grabbed a plastic chair that caught Issa's weight just before her knees gave out. "I am not—"

Adam? Party? Cat Morena's neck?

Issa counted to ten and hoped she was dreaming. "But— Oh. I feel dizzy."

She replayed the events of the weekend over in her head. Adam calling her at 8:00 p.m. on Friday night to tell her he wasn't feeling too hot and wouldn't be able to join them at the movies. Did he sound sick then? Her mind was too foggy to remember. But then, after she'd gotten home, she'd dialed his cell phone to check on him. He hadn't answered.

But he was sick! He was probably asleep, nitwit, her mind argued back.

"Okay, guys, let's think about this. Like, logically." Gigi interrupted her thoughts. "Ishaan got this news from the Athens Gossip Mill. Maybe it's a miscommunication type of thing. You know what happens when couples don't communicate, right? Remember in *The O.C.* when Marissa didn't tell Ryan about

Trey attacking her? Then Ryan thought they were doing it and he got so pissed and—"

"Bottom line, Iz. Is this something Adam would do?" Ishaan, thankfully, cut Gigi off. "If it's true, I'll kill him." Ishaan rolled up the sleeves of his button-down and slammed his left fist into his right hand. "He's dead. What would he want with that psycho bitch?"

Well, Issa knew what Adam would want from Cat. What every other guy in school wanted. Cat wasn't called "La Cuerpa" for no reason. If this rumor was even true, that is.

The real question was what Cat wanted with *Adam*. It wasn't enough that Cat had already had the homecoming princess title, an accent guys were gaga over, more money than Britney Spears could dream of and a body every girl in school would give up their trust funds for. But now she wanted Adam Mitchell? Nerdy, band-geek Adam.

Not possible.

This rumor was getting too stupid to even make the rounds. Issa was going to put an end to it immediately.

"I need to talk to him. He'll tell me the truth." Issa stood up.

Ishaan muttered something and Gigi gave him a sharp look. "That's a good idea, Iz. I mean, if he wasn't there, then…"

Issa stopped listening. Adam! She saw his familiar

silhouette close a locker door and pile his books up high in the hallway.

"There he is! Gotta go." She dashed out of the classroom and into the crowded hallway. Her friends were still standing in the chem lab, concerned expressions on their faces.

Adam was going to be so pissed when he heard the rumor. Maybe it was time the two of them confronted Cat and told her to go to hell once and for all.

"Hey." Issa wrapped her arms around Adam's bony back, ignoring her usual "no PDA" rule. It felt so good to hold him after her horrendous afternoon.

"Issa, hey. Uh, what's up?" He gave her a strange smile and pushed his tortoiseshell glasses up his nose.

"Argh." She slipped her hand into his. "I had a crazy afternoon. What about you? How was the test? Do you feel better?"

"Yeah. Much."

"Are you all recovered from your cold?"

"Uh, yeah. I got a lot of rest over the weekend, so…"

There it was. Adam probably lay around the whole weekend in his room nursing his cold and missing her. She should have stopped by. Poor baby.

Issa sidestepped a gothic freshman couple making out against the lockers and glanced away enviously. She and Adam used to be like that. Of course, not in a public hallway for the whole school to see, but they had gotten pretty hot and heavy in Adam's car after home-coming earlier that year—till they were interrupted so rudely by passing headlights anyway. Issa smiled. That had been a good night. She couldn't wait till prom to complete what they had started that night....

Lately, school had gotten so busy she felt like they'd started to take each other for granted. Felt like the only thing they got together to do anymore was study—actually study—not sneak kisses while Adam's mom was downstairs.

Issa sighed. They had to get back to being crazy and in love again. Like that morning. It had been ages since Adam had surprised her with flowers. She needed to just be honest with Adam and confess what was bothering her. It was the first step.

"Hey, listen. Thought you should know." Issa hesitated. Should she even tell him? Oh, why not? They would get a good laugh about it and she could finally put it behind her. "There's this weird rumor going on about you and Cat Morena, and I, uh, wanted to ask you about it."

She expected Adam to laugh and tell her he would never have anything to do with a ditz like Cat. Instead, he frowned.

"Iz, I really needed to talk to you about something on Friday, but I didn't get the chance."

Why didn't he deny the rumor?

"Oh...okay." Issa stopped. She wasn't sure she liked his tone.

"Hey, Adam." A group of guys with broad football-player shoulders came by and clapped Adam on the back. "Going to Sunshine's party this weekend?"

"Uh, yeah..." The freckles popped out on Adam's nose. He nervously ran his fingers through his dirty blond hair.

The football-player crowd was actually taking the time to talk to Adam. Not to mention he was invited to one of Sunshine's parties. Sunshine Harris, Queen of the Nasty Cheerleaders. Cat Morena's best friend, Skipper twin number two. No...this wasn't possible.

Issa watched as Adam made small talk with the jocks. What *did* he have in common with them? It certainly wasn't a love of academia.

Issa and Adam were at the top of their class, always competing for the coveted number-one spot that all Ivy League colleges looked at. They'd started off as study buddies during their freshman year and soon were spending every waking hour together, cramming biology and trigonometry into their heads, leaving no time for a social life. So when Adam had asked her to go to their freshman-year homecoming dance as his date, Issa was thrilled. With a roundish body, ragged hair and acne-prone skin, Issa knew she was no grand beauty and was happy just to be asked.

That was the night she realized that skinny, shy Adam cleaned up very nicely and her heart actually sped up when he held her in his arms for a slow dance. She wasn't surprised when he kissed her at her door that night. It just seemed so right.

And it had been that way for the past two years. Until now. Issa looked hard at her boyfriend. He was going to parties and not bothering to mention it to her. What next?

"So, uh, you're going to Sunshine's this weekend?" Issa felt the dread start to rise again as they walked away from the football players. "Were you at a party last weekend by any chance?"

Suddenly she didn't want to know. She wished she could take the words back and live in her dreamworld for just a bit longer.

"Actually, that's what I wanted to talk to you about. Look." He stopped and pulled her into a quiet corner as a flood of band students paraded by with their tubas and trombones.

That's when Issa knew everything was about to change. Adam had been acting weird the past two weeks, but she had attributed his behavior to worrying about midterms.

"You're great, Iz, but sometimes I wonder why we're together. Don't you think that maybe, you know…"

"I don't know what you're trying to say. So I suggest you come right out and say it and quit stallin'." Her voice was growing high and she had an idea of what was going to happen next. This was Adam, *her* Adam. And he was breaking up with her. This couldn't be real. She felt like she was having an out-of-body experience.

Adam glanced around the hallway. A few people were staring at them. Issa realized the stricken look on her face was probably giving away what was going on in that corner. "I just need to find who I am. Before high school is over. I don't want to be this…nerd forever. I want to know who else I can become."

"What's wrong with who you are now?"

"I—we, ever since we started high school, we got into this routine and we've never tried anything new. Every day's the same. Classes, study dates, movies on Saturdays, debates. That's it. We can go through another two years of high school like this, or we can try something different."

Issa knew what he was trying to say, but she held on to some hope. "So we'll both change. We'll go to football games, parties, all that stuff—"

"No. That wouldn't be different."

Everything was perfect. Cat Morena had once

again swept into her life and turned everything inside out. Issa felt a burning hatred for Cat like she'd never felt before. "Different. You mean me. You can just say it. You don't want me anymore."

"It's just that—I can't be with you and expect to change my life. It's always going to be the same and—"

"We're over," Issa stated in a steady voice, even though just saying the words shot a ten-pound stone into the center of her belly. "Who is she? Who is going to help you make over your life?"

"There's no one—"

Yeah, she knew very well who it was. "Cat Morena? You were doing Jell-O shots off her neck as far as I hear."

"How did you—"

So it was true. He didn't even try to deny his lying and cheating.

"God, Adam. What the hell are you doing? The Cat Morenas of this world are only going to toy with you, then throw you away. She wants a modeling contract and some millionaire boyfriend to take care of her, not you!"

Adam was silent.

"Say something, you little freak!" Issa practically shrieked. Now everyone was openly staring at them, but she didn't care.

Before he could respond, a hush fell over the hallway as Cat and her cronies made their way through the crowd. When the three of them spotted Issa and Adam, Cat turned her head and whispered something to Sunshine Harris. Then they both giggled while Cat shot Issa an evil smile.

"She's such a bitch. A horrible snake," Issa muttered, her fear of Cat evaporating. She didn't care anymore if Cat overheard. What did Issa have left to lose now?

Adam glanced away from Issa and toward the girls. He fidgeted with the strap of his backpack and untied one shoelace with his other foot. "Every guy wants her. And she likes me. She appreciates me, and she never tries to one-up me. Not like you."

Issa felt the tears start to well up in her eyes. That was what this whole thing was about? That was how he got seduced by Cat's charms? Because Cat made him feel *smart?* Cat could make a toadstool feel smart. This was not an accomplishment!

"I thought that was just a joke between us. I was just playin'. I thought all that 'top two people in class' was just for kicks."

Issa could feel her old downtown Detroit "don't take crap from anyone" attitude creeping in and she didn't give a damn. When she'd just moved to New Joliet, she'd gotten made fun of for being from "the ghetto" by all the popular girls. All they'd wanted to hear about was gang wars and shootings. No one had cared about the rich African-American heritage Detroit had produced or the incredible automotive industry that was housed in the city. She'd buried her past deep down and become the East Coast brainiac everyone expected her to be and never mentioned her roots again.

"Well, it wasn't fun for me," Adam said quietly. "I don't want a girlfriend who goes around telling everyone how much smarter she is than me. You may be smart, but that's all you are, Issa. Brains don't make a complete person!"

That did it. The tears started spilling from her eyes. She swiped at her cheek with her shoulder. "Oh, my being smart didn't seem to bother you last night when you called crying in desperation!"

Adam didn't say anything. Apparently saving his ass in a moment of crisis wasn't as important as looking hot in a pair of Seven Jeans. Suddenly Issa felt like everything she knew about the world was wrong. Intelligent girls—zero. Slutty girls—ten points. "Forget it, you slimy little jackass. I hope you realize someday how much I appreciated you and how you'll never have that again."

Issa threw her head back and swept past Cat and her entourage with as much dignity as she could muster. She pretended not to hear their tinkling laughter behind her as she walked steadily into the girls' room. She was proud she'd been able to contain her sobbing until she was safely in the stall.

How could this be happening? They had just celebrated their two-year anniversary last week! The whole world knew they were together and how crazy she was about him. How could she go out in public and tell people that Adam had suddenly stopped loving her?

All Issa wanted was to go home. Hide in her bed until this nightmare ended. But by the sounds of lockers slamming shut and tennis shoes squeaking, she knew the hallways weren't clear yet. No, she couldn't get out of this hell until she was sure everyone was gone.

How would she ever be able to face Adam again with Cat Morena by his side?

two

Men, Chocolate and Coffee Are All Better Rich

"I'm fine. Let's just stop talking about it, huh?" Issa, nestled into a mound of hand-embroidered pillows, glowered up at the ceiling. She knew if she met Ishaan's sad puppy eyes, she would burst into tears.

"Iz," Ishaan said, then reached over and tousled her ripply hair. "Do you want me to beat his ass? You know I will."

Tempting, but what good would it do? Adam would still be in love with Cat Morena and Issa would still be the laughingstock of the school. Cat had won again. Except this time, Issa didn't understand what she'd done to Cat and what Cat was really after. She refused to believe Cat had suddenly and painfully fallen in love with Adam Mitchell, the boy who in eighth grade was voted Most Likely to Host *Star Trek* Conventions in His Garage.

"Should I take that as a 'Yes, Ishaan, my hero, please beat up that jackass for me'?" Ishaan asked, his eyes twinkling.

Issa smiled despite the hideousness of the day. He always knew how to make her feel better. "Don't beat his ass," she sighed. Ishaan played tennis and had a mean left hook. No matter how pissed she was at Adam at the moment, she didn't want him hurt.

"What reason did he give for ending it? And don't tell me he said it was because Cat was hotter than you."

Issa flinched. Well, pretty much that was exactly what he said. But she was ashamed to admit to Ishaan that her now ex-boyfriend found her to be intelligent yet repulsive to look at.

"He gave me some lame-ass reason about him being a nerd and me holding him back from being cool." She rolled her eyes as dramatically as she could. "Yeah, that was me all along. Anyway, it doesn't matter." Issa pushed Ishaan's hand away from her hair. "Let him do what he wants. He weighs ninety-five pounds, let's see if he can ever do anything *but* be a nerd."

The pink and purple saris Issa had hung on her windows shuddered gently in the breeze. Today, even hiding in the ethnic lair that was her bedroom wasn't comforting to her. The *Om*-printed jasmine candles, and prints of the Taj Mahal and Jaipur on the walls weren't taking her away to another world like they usually did.

Let's see how soon Cat dumps him on his ass. She continued to glare at the ceiling.

After she and her mother had moved into this place, Issa had stood on a ladder, painted the ceiling navy blue and glued on glow-in-the-dark moons. She'd thought they were the coolest things in the world and whenever she had friends over, she would turn off the lights to show off her mini solar system. Now they seemed like childish plastic blobs. *She* felt like a childish plastic blob.

"Is there anything I can do? Slash his tires? Get the soccer team together and paint 'male whore' on this garage door? Wouldn't that be a *Desperate House-wives* moment?"

Issa almost laughed at the thought. Even though Ishaan was one of the more popular members of the senior class and a star on the soccer and tennis teams, he was the most loyal friend she had. And usually she would tease him about his closeted *Desperate House-wives* addiction, but she didn't feel like it today. "There's no reason to do anything. I'm over it. He's a fool. Not spending another moment thinking about him. Okay? No more."

"You mean that?" To her annoyance, Ishaan sounded amused, and not a least bit convinced.

Issa sighed. Ishaan knew her too well. His family was one of two other Indian families in New Joliet and the Banerjees had taken Alisha under their wing and acted as if the Mazumders were blood relatives, despite Issa's half-and-half status.

Alisha's parents and the Banerjees were from the same city of Calcutta in India. Even though Alisha didn't speak Bengali with Issa or her older brother, Amir, plus the fact that she was estranged from her superconservative parents, she still carried her heritage and encouraged her children to do the same.

And ever since Amir had moved to Los Angeles for school, Ishaan had taken it upon himself to look out for Issa as if she was his own little sister. Sometimes it drove her crazy, but today she was happy he'd insisted on coming over and sitting with her.

"Can we change the subject?" Issa asked. "I don't want to waste another moment on this. He deserves everything that's coming to him."

"Of course," Ishaan said. "You're completely over him, right?" he repeated. "Never going to think of him again."

"That's right."

"Good. Great. How about we—"

"Dumped for Cat Morena!" Issa burst out. "It had

to be Cat Morena! The one person I can't stand on this whole earth! Girl thinks baklava comes out of volcanoes. So she drives a Lotus and wears those trashy four-inch-heeled boots that cost more than our mortgage. Is that really so great? You're a guy, Ishaan, do you think she's all that?"

"Uh—"

Issa hurried on, afraid to hear his answer. "And who invites every guy she dates over for a 'dip' in her dad's hot tub? She's a tramp!"

"But you're over him, remember?"

Issa gritted her teeth and stewed. She was over him. A smart girl like her was never again going to be hung up on some guy. She wasn't a typical moronic teenager and certainly wasn't going to start acting like one now. And if Adam was stupid enough to believe whatever Cat had told him, well, he definitely wasn't the Adam she had loved.

"I don't care what he does," she said. "I just always thought Adam would be too smart to fall for *those* kinds of girls." She realized she sounded petty, stupid…and jealous. But she had to let it all out. "Whatever. Let him have his fun. I give him a week before he comes crawling back. Then I'll be the one having fun. Hmm, how many ways can you say, 'go to hell'? I'll tell him in other languages. Do we have an international thesaurus up in here?"

"Iz—" Ishaan was interrupted by the Maroon 5 ring tone of Issa's cell phone. She swore she saw a hint of a smile on his lips as he handed over the phone. "Here. I gotta go anyway. Gigi said she'd stop by and see you after cheer practice."

"Don't laugh at me!" she yelled as Ishaan left the room. "I'm over him. I hate him. If this is him, I'll give him a piece of my mind."

"It's your mom. She's picking you up for some surprise, remember?" Ishaan paused in her doorway. "Go out and have fun. This day can't get any worse, right?"

"This better be a good surprise, Mama," Issa said, sliding into the passenger side of Alisha's rust-colored Toyota Corolla. "I'm really not in the mood today."

Alisha tapped the steering wheel in tune to the radio, the silver bangles on her wrists jangling. "I think you'll like this one, oh favorite daughter."

Hmph. Alisha's teasing. Never a care in the world for Alisha. Sometimes Issa swore she was the mother and Alisha the daughter. Times like this it annoyed her. Why couldn't she have a normal mother? One who fed her chicken soup and let her hide under the covers for a week.

"Whatever." Issa sighed and faced out the passenger-side window.

"Hey, kiddo, are you okay?" Alisha asked, turning Issa's chin toward her. "Have you been crying?"

Issa hesitated. Right now she just wanted to stop thinking about it. If Issa started on the pity party now, Alisha would be furious with Adam. She would threaten to kick his sorry ass. And the surprise would be ruined.

I'll tell her afterward, Issa decided. "No, I'm fine. Don't want to talk about it right now."

Alisha still looked concerned. "You sure, babe? We can do this later if you want."

"No, no. I—never mind. What's this surprise about? Are we going somewhere fancy?" Issa studied Alisha's outfit. She'd changed clothes after work. The starched blue blouse and gray pencil skirt her mother was wearing was a far cry from her usual floor-length skirts and peasant tops. Her normally wavy hair was straightened and pulled neatly back at the nape of her neck. Issa became aware she was in jeans and a ragged hoodie sweatshirt, her shoulder-length curls now in a messy bun. She was *not* dressed for a night out.

"You're dressed up! Are we finally going to see *Joseph and the Amazing Technicolor Dreamcoat?* Mom! I'm not dressed for the theater!"

"Issa, I can assure you with my strongest conviction that we would *not* be going to the theater on a Monday night." Alisha attempted to start the car. The engine huffed and shut off.

"Well, I never know with you." Issa was still suspicious. "Remember that time we took a bus to the Hamptons just to sell seashells by the seashore?"

"I was young and you were silly then," Alisha said, her crescent-shaped lips curving as the engine finally groaned to life.

"It was last year!"

"And wasn't it fun? A good surprise?"

"Yes," Issa admitted. Any adventure with Alisha at the helm was fun. She was not your usual conservative Indian-American mother. Raised by overly strict parents, she had run away from home, married someone handsome and inappropriate, had Issa and her brother soon after and had never really grown up. Alisha had vowed years ago to raise Issa right, in a way her own parents had never done with her.

Issa and Alisha had always shared everything: size 6 clothes, the same hazel eyes, a taste for coconut lattes and sweet tea, and secrets. Until today. Issa wondered what all the hush-hush was about. She watched the neighborhoods change from middle class to upper crust as the car whizzed through New Joliet.

Ten minutes later Alisha pulled into a circular driveway topped by a three-story mansion.

"What's this? Did we win the lottery? Is this our new house?"

Alisha laughed. "You'll see."

Issa had been joking, but Alisha's smile was so happy, for a second she thought it might be possible.

Alisha rang the doorbell with Issa hanging behind a few steps.

"*Buenas tardes,* Alisha." A formidable salt-and-pepper-haired man, fully suited down to polished loafers, answered the door in a slightly accented voice. "I'm so glad Issa was able to make it."

Diego.

Alisha had been casually dating the slick, overly polished man for a few months. Thankfully, Issa hadn't had too many run-ins with him. *He* was the surprise? This had to be his house. Alisha normally had fun taste in men—tormented artists who were consumed by their genius or wannabe comedians who considered the world their stage. True, the relationships never lasted more than a month, but Issa knew her mother was just enjoying life. It wasn't as if she was looking for her soul mate. Issa's daddy was still out there somewhere and she knew her mama could never be with anyone else for long.

But this Diego was different. Issa had heard he was rich, but apparently he was superrich. The expensive-looking suits, the fancy corporate lawyer job, this vulgarly large house. So ridiculous. He looked like a clean-cut Antonio Banderas, and sounded like him, too. Not Alisha's style at all.

"I'm so glad you came tonight for dinner, Issa." Diego reached out to take Issa's zipped-up hoodie.

"Oh, yeah," she muttered and shoved her fingers into her sweatshirt pockets. She wasn't about to reveal the ribbed Hindu-god-imprinted tank top she wore underneath.

"My young daughter will be joining us tonight. She is most anxious to meet you." Diego either ignored, or didn't understand, Issa's sullen attitude.

"Wonderful," Issa said through her teeth. Could this day really get much worse? She didn't know Diego's bratty kid and didn't particularly care to after the horrendous day she'd had.

She surreptitiously checked out the house as Diego hung up Alisha's coat. Wow. White marble everything. Spiral staircase, burgundy carpeting. It was like something out of a design magazine. And all of this for just Diego and his kid? It was a far cry from her and Alisha's run-down town house with mismatched garage-sale furniture.

A small movement caught Issa's eyes and she noticed a girl sauntering down the spiral staircase. A tiny smirk on her lips, the girl made her way to the base of the stairs, her narrow hips creating figure eights as she walked, her silky hair swishing around her waist of her white dress. Not just any girl. Cat Morena.

Issa heard a strange gurgling sound in her throat. Cat Morena was Diego's daughter? It couldn't be! Was she being "punked"?

The wicked smile Cat shot Issa assured her this was no dream. She was real. Deadly real.

"Catalina, meet Issa, Alisha's daughter. I am sure you two have seen each other at school, yes?" Diego kissed his daughter's outstretched hand.

"Of course, *Papi*. Issa and I have some common friends. Adam, right?" Cat said the words so sweetly, Issa almost believed the innocent tone herself. "We were just talking about her last weekend while studying."

Studying? Yeah, he was studying your a— "Girl, I think you were doing a lot more than studying!" Issa spat before she could stop herself.

"Issa!" Alisha looked shocked. "What on earth…"

Anger took over her words and Issa felt herself starting to lose control. "Adam and I broke up. And it's because of—"

"Adam was not good enough for you. Not to worry, *chica*. He'll get what he deserves," Cat said in a reassuring voice. "Alisha, tell your daughter. Those high-school boys, so fickle. One day they are yours, the next, going after someone prettier and more popular."

What the hell kind of game was she playing? How

did she manage to make every insult sound like a compliment? "I—"

"We should sit," Diego interrupted, looking over at Alisha. Pity, he looked as if he had no idea of the kind of activities that went on up in his house.

Dip in the hot tub, anyone?

Issa seethed and remembered Cat's words this morning.

Off to help your mummy scrub the floors.

Oooh, when Alisha found out, Diego would get hell. That would put an end to this screwed-up relationship.

"It is such an honor to finally have you here for dinner, *Professora!*" Cat practically purred, taking Alisha's arm and leading her to the living room with Issa dragging her feet behind.

She was going to ignore Cat, get through this dinner and never speak to her mother again.

"Call me Alisha. Please." Alisha smiled at Cat, earning a scornful look from Issa.

Diego and Alisha sat next to each other on a white leather couch, with Cat taking the ottoman. That left the love seat on which Issa perched, trying to edge as far away from the Morenas as possible.

The leather couch was sticking to her pants. She gingerly pulled her low-rise jeans up, the squeaking noise attracting Cat's attention.

"Is that a tattoo?" Cat said in an overly loud voice.

Knowing Cat, she was hoping Alisha didn't know and Issa would get busted for it.

Diego stopped talking and glanced over at Issa with a frown.

Issa quickly pulled her sweatshirt down over the *Om* tattoo on her hip. The previous year she'd been obsessed with Sanskrit, the ancient Indian language, and had half joked she would love to have the symbol of peace imprinted on her to remind herself to keep her cool through the crazy teenage years. To her surprise, Alisha had agreed to let Issa get the tattoo on her sixteenth birthday and had even gotten one herself.

"Iz and I got matching ones." Alisha raised her blouse to show Cat her own tattoo. "Cool, huh?"

"Yeah." Cat looked awestruck.

Diego looked horrified.

Issa could feel herself smiling. Hopefully now Alisha would see how ill-fit she and Diego were. It was like Gwen Stefani dating Donald Trump.

Or maybe not. Diego resumed his serene smile and put his arm around Alisha as if he had no problem dating a woman who let her sixteen-year-old daughter permanently scar herself. "So, Catalina, Issa, how were your days at school today?"

Issa pointedly stared out the window in the living room at the darkened sky. Ugh, she could see Diego's and Alisha's reflections in the window.

Diego bent his head over Alisha's and whispered something. Alisha bit her lip, then nodded slowly. They both broke into smiles. What were they sniggering about now?

"Issa, Diego specifically asked to have dinner with you tonight so you could meet Catalina."

She knew Catalina well enough, thanks.

"I have a feeling you two would make fine friends." Diego smiled at both girls. Issa inched even farther away from Cat. The girl could poison her right here in front of their parents without even batting her big fake eyelashes.

"Yeah, sure," Issa said instead. The sooner this pompous snob stopped talking, the better.

"Your mother says you have adjusted well at Athens."

Issa paused. Adjusted well. Right. She was the only student in the whole school whose parents weren't millionaires…and everyone knew it. The only ones who didn't care were Ishaan and Gigi. If it weren't for them, Issa would have spent the rest of her high-school years playing second tier to a bunch of spoiled East Coast princesses. Girls like Cat. Issa's cheeks started to burn again. It just wasn't fair. How could a horrible witch like Cat have everything? Money, friends, a fancy convertible…and now Adam. She hated Cat, hated her with every fiber of her soul.

"Why don't you come with me, Iz? We can fetch drinks for the parents?" Catalina asked sweetly, turning to Issa, her velvet eyes widening.

Fetch drinks? What was this, a bad fifties movie?

"Dinner's almost ready, *mi hija*. Don't keep us waiting," Diego called behind them.

"Of course not, *Papi*."

Issa reluctantly followed Catalina, while glancing over her shoulder at her mother. Alisha and Diego were gazing at each other, Diego gently stroking her arm. Gross.

They had to get out of here. For good. Her mother could never see Diego again. Unfortunately, her mother looked happy and Diego was treating her like a queen. And Cat was acting as if she'd gotten a personality transplant overnight.

Issa had her work cut out for her.

Catalina led Issa into a room that was less kitchen and more futuristic space station. She immediately started throwing open cabinets and pulled out a tiny shot glass and a bottle of Sprite. "I need good vodka to get through this dinner."

As soon as Cat took the top off the bottle, the strong smell of alcohol permeated the room.

Vodka in a Sprite bottle? Now, that was just ghetto.

Issa stood openmouthed and watched as Catalina poured herself a shot of the liquid, threw it into

the back of her throat. "Actually I need two."
Repeat.

"What the—" Issa should have known better than
to trust Cat for even a moment.

"What, what're you going to do? Huh, *chica?* Tell
Daddy on me?" Catalina sneered. "Please. I know
how to handle him, okay? Don't get any ideas."

"Yeah, I bet."

"Yeah, whatever." Catalina carefully restashed her
alcoholic paraphernalia and pulled a tin of Altoids
from the same shelf. "I don't know what kind of
game you and your brown-trash mom are playing."

Issa resisted the urge to slap Cat. "What the hell
did you say? You think we want to be here? If your
idiot of a father—"

"He's having some sort of midlife crisis obviously.
Don't worry, your mother isn't that special."

Cat swallowed two Altoids and breathed into her
hand. Apparently satisfied that the alcoholic scent
was gone, she hid the box of mints. "He's decided he's
going to be with her. I don't care. Up to him. But I'll
tell you this." Cat stepped very close to Issa, all signs
of innocence gone from her almond-shaped eyes.
"One day when he realizes he's brought home
mulatto trash, you'll be at the end of the driveway
with the rest of the garbage."

Issa's brain raced. Diego was just playing Alisha.

He had no idea about her background or ex-husband. When he found out, this stupid love affair would be over so fast...

Cat brushed past Issa, shoving her shoulder into Issa's collarbone. "Get in the dining room. Smile. Act happy. Oh, and if you get in my way and think you can tattle on me to my dad, good luck. You think I made your life hell before? No, *chica,* that was nothing. You'll see exactly what I'm capable of."

Issa rubbed her bruised collar. The little tramp was pretty strong.

Cat swept into the dining room and Issa could practically hear her go through her Jekyll and Hyde transformation. "Issa's on her way," Cat announced sweetly.

Issa seethed. How could Alisha possibly think she and Cat would ever get along? The girl was evil, pure evil.

Dinner was torture. Diego had crafted a fine leg of lamb stewed in a tomato-and-onion curry served over white rice with a side of black beans. Any other day, Issa would have gobbled down such a gourmet meal. But today, it tasted like a *Fear Factor* delicacy in her mouth.

She avoided Cat's eyes while the girl jabbered on about school and friends. Issa finally managed to swallow a few bites of food and pushed her plate away. It was almost over. As soon as they got home, Issa would explain everything to her mother. Surely, she would break up with Diego immediately and inform him of what a tramp his daughter was.

Issa peeked over at Cat's dish to see what anorexics ate nowadays. Surprisingly, Cat was chowing down on her leg of lamb and her plate was almost clean. Issa rolled her eyes. She wouldn't be surprised if Cat "excused herself" in about ten minutes to go to the bathroom and puke it all up.

"There's something...we'd like to discuss with you." The hesitation in Alisha's voice made Issa sit up straight from her half-slouchy pose. The "you tell her" expressions Alisha and Diego were exchanging did not look like good news.

"Issa, last weekend, I asked your mother to marry me."